I'

a pair of wanderers from the Waking
World, Hero and Eldin, are faced with
powers out of time, forces that can
spell the end of the Dreamlands,
the real world, perhaps the
entire universe:

CTHULHU!

*'For when the First Ones sought to
ascertain the truth of the olden myths – whether
or not Cthulhu and certain of his contemporaries
indeed lived on – then they recoiled in horror
from that which they discovered: namely that
the legends did not lie!
Cthulhu lived – he lives! – and he will
never cease in his efforts to free himself from
magic-forged chains and roam free again
in the sane and ordered universe,
breeding Madness and Ruin
and Horror and
Chaos!'*

Hero of Dreams

Brian Lumley

HEADLINE

ISBN 0 7472 3301 2

Typeset in 10/11 pt English Times
by Colset Private Limited, Singapore

Printed and bound in Great Britain by
Collins, Glasgow

HEADLINE BOOK PUBLISHING PLC
Headline House
79 Great Titchfield Street
London W1P 7FN

For June,
who goes outside
and does it anywhere

CONTENTS

PART ONE

PART TWO

PART THREE

PART FOUR

PART FIVE

EPILOGUE

My own dreams being particularly vivid and real – to such an extent that I never know for sure whether or not I am dreaming until I wake up – I would not like to argue which world is the more vital: the waking world or the world of dream. Certainly the waking world seems the more solid; but consider what science tells us about the atomic make-up of so-called solids – and what are you left with . . .?

– Gerhard Schrach.

PART ONE

PART ONE

I
FIRST MEETING

It was evening and the uplands of dream were turning chilly. Spiked grasses nodded in a slight breeze, like hissing Gorgon heads, where they made silhouettes atop rocky rises. Soon the sun would be down and the stars would come out to blaze in the heavens of Earth's dreamland. David Hero did not know these parts, for his dreams had never before carried him here; he knew only that he did not like this place, where green plains gave way to scrub, stony slopes and sliding shale, and the crags cast gaunt shadows that would soon become threatening caves of blackness as night drew in.

He shivered a little and fondled the hilt of his curved sword where it hung at his hip, then turned up the hood of his brown cape a little – but not too much. He did not want to shut out the evening sounds of these uplands, for his ears were sensitive and would often tell him of a danger before the danger itself became visible. The breeze stiffened to a wind and moaned with an eerie insistence as he leaned forward up the slope, and high overhead a scud of gray clouds hurried into view as they crossed the peaks and headed south.

South . . .

Now why couldn't he have dreamed himself south?

3

To Celephais, perhaps, where King Kuranes reigned, or sky-floating Serannian where the west wind flows into the sky? But no, he was here, wherever here was, and so must accept whichever dreams were his due this night. Whichever dreams . . . or nightmares.

David Hero knew he was in the north of Earth's dreamland, but no more than that. These peaks above him could well be the ultimate range leading to Leng itself, whose plateau was home to some of dreamland's vilest inhabitants; or they might merely be the foothills of that far mightier escarpment, Kadath in the Cold Waste. Thoughts such as these had almost determined the dreamer to turn back and head for healthier lands when, on cresting a ridge, he came upon a scene which had him drawing his sword in a whisper of steel and falling automatically into a defensive crouch.

Below, a lone wanderer sought cover in crevices of rock; while ranged about him, a trio of six-legged spider-hounds hissed and snapped at his leather-clad legs, trying to secure a hold on him and pull him down. One of them awkwardly clutched a straight sword in a prehensile forepaw, having doubtless snatched it from the frantically scrabbling, hoarsely panting object of their detestable torture.

David Hero knew some of the ways of spider-hounds from tales told to him by travellers and storytellers in dreamland's more civilized regions: how they would wear a man down with their vile hissing and leaping, then paralyze him with their poisonous stings and eat him alive, often making their meal last through several nights. Such was obviously the intention of this monstrous trio, and Hero could well understand the near-demented scrabbling of their victim as he sought to find some crevice in which to wedge himself, the better to make a stand against the horrors.

Without a thought to his own safety, the newcomer

gritted his teeth and went slithering and leaping in the gloom down the shale-covered slope. He waved his sword above his head as he ran at the hissing, scampering creatures, whistling and shouting like a madman. Still on the run, he snatched up a large lump of lava in his free hand and hurled it at the insect-like hounds, and had the satisfaction of seeing one of them leap high in the air with the shock of the impact as the missile struck home.

Then he was upon them, slicing with his sword and panting through clenched teeth and grimacing lips. By good fortune his singing blade took the jointed hind legs right off one of them – the one that held aloft the beleaguered stranger's sword – and in another moment the man had leaped forward to snatch back his weapon from the crippled spider-hound. Striking together, the two men put paid to that demented creature where it dragged its stinger uselessly behind it.

But now the other spider-hounds had realized that the balance of the game had evened up, and that therefore a quick end must be made of it. As at a single word of command they launched themselves at Hero, twisting their bodies in the air so that their stingers struck at his face. He ducked, impaled one of them on his sword, felt the weight of the other on his back and a lancing agony as a single drop of mordant poison burned through his clothing to the skin . . . then felt the horror kicked from him and heard its final hiss as the rescued man took both hands to his sword and hacked its cockroach head clean from its body.

Quickly, without a backward glance, Hero tugged his own weapon free of the scale-armored hound where it twitched and jerked among shale and lava fragments, then split its chitinous skull with a single stroke. The fight was finished, and only the moaning

of the wind over the peaks remained: that and the
panting of the men, and the nameless drip of the thin
gray ichor which was the life-blood of these denizens
of nightmare.

Now Hero turned to the other man, peering at him
where he stood cleaning his weapon on his black
jacket. The other looked back in turn, and gratitude
shone in his eyes; but his breathing was ragged and he
coughed painfully.

'They took you by surprise,' Hero ventured.

'Eh?' the other finally grunted. 'Yes, they did.
Damned horrors! Didn't see 'em till they were on me.
They don't hiss at all when they're tracking you –
only when they have you cornered!'

'I wouldn't know,' Hero answered. 'This is the first
time I've come across them – I'm happy to say!' He
touched a severed head with his fur-booted foot and
turned it until starlight fell onto the faceted eyes, then
grimaced at the way the thing seemed to stare at him
even in death.

Then, headless as it was, one of the carcasses began
to twitch and the hard carapace rattled on the rocks.
Both men stepped back from the dead things and
shivered – and not alone from the chill of the night
air. Finally they turned more fully to one another and
clasped hands in the manner of dreamland.

'In the village where I sometimes lodge, I'm known
as Eldin,' the dark-jacketed man told Hero. 'Since
Eldin is the old word for "wanderer," it suits me well
enough. Of course, I've another name in the waking
world . . . at least, I think I have. And how are you
called?'

'My name's Hero, David Hero. I haven't earned
myself a dream-name yet, though I'm pretty well-
travelled in the better known places.'

'No dream-name, eh, David?' Eldin grinned and

nodded as if he knew something special. 'Just a fellow traveller from the waking world, eh? Well, there seem to be damn few of us about these days. And what brings you here?'

'I could ask the same of you,' Hero answered, casting nervously about. 'And I would if I didn't think this a funny sort of spot to be spending our time in idle chatter. Is there no place we can make ourselves at ease for the night?'

'I was making for a cave back there in the shadows when these damned things set on me,' Eldin said. 'I've a flint in my pocket and the makings in my pack, and we should be able to pick up a few dry sticks for a fire. What would you say to a cup of tea?' Hero caught a flash of grinning teeth in the darkness.

'I'd say that was a very kind offer,' he answered. 'Lead on, Eldin, and we'll pick up some sticks as we go.'

'Now then,' said Eldin when they sat on flat stones in a dry and sheltered cave and sipped their tea out of tiny silver cups, 'you were going to tell me what you're doing here, on these unbeaten paths so far away from dreamland's towns and cities.'

Hero shrugged. 'I go where dreams take me. This time they brought me here.'

'You're not an inveterate dreamer, then?'

'Well I am, yes, but my dreaming never seems to have much point to it – if you know what I mean. It's like I said: I go wherever my dreams take me. I have no anchor here, as you seem to have. No village where I board, no place to call home. I never seem to be here long enough to build up any sort of permanency. Come to think of it, I believe I'm pretty much the same in the waking world. When I'm there I can't remember much of this place, and when I'm here . . .'

7

'You can't remember much of the other place, eh?'

'Only my name,' Hero answered, 'and that's about all.'

'I always make a point,' the other said, 'of going down the seven hundred steps to the Gate of Deeper Slumber. I've found that if you do that it makes it easier to stay here for longer periods. You don't wake up so easy. Those steps take you down to lower levels of dream, if you see what I mean.'

'Not for me,' Hero shook his head. 'I've heard of people using those steps who never returned to the waking world at all. They're used by people who *have* to escape into dreams, and I don't have to. I suppose I'm not much of a dreamer, really – and I don't think I really care to be.'

'Have it your own way,' Eldin growled. 'Anyway, we still seem to be two of a sort. The way I see it, we've got too much going for us in the waking world – or too little – and so we dream. You say you've no anchor here? I'll bet there's precious little to anchor you to the waking world, either. And then again I'm older than you. Perhaps dreams are kinder to me than the waking world. Anyhow, I like it here. Things seem easier, somehow.' He coughed and held up a great hand to his mouth. 'I'll take my chances in dreams. If they don't kill me, this damned old troublesome body of mine surely will!'

Hero shrugged. He looked at the other in the flickering firelight. Eldin was older than Hero's twenty-six years by at least a dozen, probably more, with a scarred, bearded, quite unhandsome face which yet sported surprisingly clear blue eyes. Stocky and heavy, yet somehow gangly, there was something almost apish about him; yet his every move and gesture hinted of exceptional intelligence and a rare strength. But Herb suspected that the man's strength

8

was being sapped internally, that the flame of death brightened steadily in his lungs, threatening to blossom into a raging inferno. Perhaps that was why he was here, this misfit from the waking world.

'And what of you?' he finally asked, seeking to confirm his reckoning. 'What are you doing here, Eldin? I mean specifically, well, *here*, in the uplands?'

Eldin grinned and sipped his tea, peering at his new friend and admiring his strong arms, clean features and straight, slim figure. 'Me? Why, I was looking for you!'

'For me?' Hero was taken aback.

'Let me explain,' said Eldin. 'In Baharna on the Isle of Oriab, there's a wharfside tavern where sailors gather from all the seas of dreamland. It's a funny little place, that tavern, and until recently none too healthy for outsiders – if you know what I mean. There's been a big clean-up, however, and many of dreamland's peoples have taken to travelling about a lot more. Even Dylath-Leen gets its quota of visitors these days, and I'm told that people are settling there again . . .'

But Eldin's words had set Hero's mind wandering. He remembered stories he'd heard of the Bad Days, when the demon-god Cthulhu's minions in dreamland had attempted a coup over all the lands of dream, and only the intervention of two men from the waking world had stopped them. He remembered the names of those men: Titus Crow and Henri-Laurent de Marigny, and felt a certain awe when he thought of the battles they had fought against all the forces of nightmare.

'Anyway,' Eldin's words brought him back to the present. 'I was in Baharna across the Southern Sea, and it was there – in this tavern I've mentioned – that my future was told by a certain seer of no mean skill. Mind you, these old bellows of mine –' (he tapped upon his great chest)'– were playing me up and I was a little drunk at the time, and so I can't swear to the surety of my memory, but still I'll tell you what I *think* the prophet told me:

'He cast his stones, gazed at my palm with his strange, invisible eyes, and said –'

'Invisible eyes?' Hero felt obliged to cut him short. 'What sort of eyes are those, for goodness' sake?'

The firelight flashed on Eldin's grin and sent shadows slithering over the cave's walls. 'What kind? Why, invisible, of course! The kind when you look into them and see . . . nothing! The spaces between the stars – an empty void – you know?'

'No,' Hero shook his head.

'You can see their edges,' Eldin patiently explained, 'Their rims, like craters on both sides of the nose – but inside them . . . Nothing! I've met several such in dreamland.'

Hero slowly nodded and said: 'You were saying?'

'Eh? Oh, yes. Well, I'd had a few drinks, I admit it – yes, and I fancy the old seer had, too – and so he read my future in the stones and in the palm of my hand. And he said:

' "Eldin, you'll meet a man one evening in the northern uplands, and he'll save your life. Then . . . He'll join you on a quest – on several quests – which will take you to the farthest corners of dreamland." '

' "Quests?" I said. "What sort of quests?" But he'd say no more.'

Fascinated, Hero asked: 'Nothing else? That was all he told you?'

'I'm afraid so,' Eldin nodded ruefully. Then he brightened and added, 'Oh, yes! He did say that if we lived through these quests, how then that you'd have earned yourself a dream-name. That's how I know you're the one.'

'Because I have no dream-name?'

Eldin nodded.

'Well then, I reckon I'll have to get along without one.'

'You won't come with me?' Eldin seemed disappointed.

'Hero by name,' the other reminded him, 'but not necessarily by inclination. And I don't much care for the way your seer foretold the future. "If" we live through it, you say? There's one sure way to live through it, my friend, and that's not to go questing in the first place! Sorry, Eldin, but you can count me out. Anyway, it all seems rather vague to me. We're to go a-questing, you say? Where to? What for?'

Eldin shrugged. 'I never did discover. But what does it matter, since you're not interested?'

Now Hero frowned. He turned his face away and gazed out of the cave's mouth into the night. 'Let's sleep on it,' he said, without looking at the other.

Eldin grinned. 'I'll take first watch,' he said.

II
DAVID HERO

David Hero awakened to sunlight that burned through his eyelids and warmed his face. He briefly wondered how this could be, for he remembered that the cave he shared with Eldin faced south and away from the rising sun. Then, shielding his eyes, he opened them to squint up at latticed windows where they sloped down and formed the east-facing roof. Through the small panes he could see the morning sun rising over Arthur's Seat.

Arthur's Seat?

Eldinburgh! Of course it was Eldinburgh. No, *Edinburgh*, without the '*l*!' Now why on Earth had he called the city Eldinburgh? And this was his studio-flat in a converted attic in the Dalkeith Road.

In that split second of confused realization, David Hero was once again a man of the waking world. All accumulated memories of that other world-life shrank and receded into those half-suspected regions of mind at which students of the human psyche have occasionally hinted and upon which they frequently conjecture. Earth's dreamland, in that moment, ceased to exist for him, or at least became a shadow in his subconscious.

Except . . .

Eldin? Now what or who in hell was Eldin? And

why had Hero been so surprised upon awakening to find himself in Edinburgh? He sat up in bed, yawned and shrugged. The mind's natural confusion in the transitory moments between dreaming and waking, he supposed. He had always had trouble waking up. Now what did he have planned for today?

A walk on the castle's esplanade? He always enjoyed that: the view of the olden city from on high. He loved the marvellous silhouettes, which always seemed to remind him of – other places, beyond memory. And perhaps that was how he might explain the inspiration for his *outré* art.

He got out of bed and crossed scrubbed floorboards to peer at yesterday's work. There, on an easel, a newly-daubed canvas was given a certain perspective as the morning light just failed to strike it. Basalt-towered and myriad-wharved, a gray and eerily fantastic city with leprous cobbled streets seemed to gloom back at him through the bleary, small-paned windows of its houses. Buckled pavements made dark-shadowed humps in subsided roads, and deserted wharves crumbled into a soulless sea. There was no sign of life at all and the whole scene was distinctly gloomy and disquieting.

Looking at the painting, Hero cocked his head on one side and frowned. The thing looked *too* damned dismal. Something utterly hideous had happened to that city, and he felt he should know what it was. He was not at all sure now that this was the effect he had wanted. There was nothing wrong with the painting itself; indeed, the work was good. No, the fault lay with the subject matter.

'Dylath-Leen,' he muttered to himself. 'Yes – but much too dreary. A good name, though!' And he picked up a pencil and quickly scrawled 'Dylath-Leen' in one corner of the canvas. 'There, now I won't forget it.'

Then he stepped back and yawned again, scratching his tousled yellow hair. The picture would be better, he thought, if done as a night scene; with dim-glowing lights behind certain of the windows, friendly groups of small people in the streets and the occasional figure on a doorstep, lanthorn held high. It would lose none of its other-worldliness, but it would certainly be made more, well – true to life? After all, Dylath-Leen was like that now . . . wasn't it?

He snorted derisively at his own fancies and turned to peer at a second, older picture where it hung in a cheap frame. This one was more lively, its highlights accentuated by the glinting sun striking into the attic room. Trapped in golden beams, motes of dust seemed to float like a thousand tiny drifting airships among faery towers, domes and turrets; and below, overhanging a blue crystal sea, the foundations of the city were set in an incredible promontory of green volcanic glass. In one corner of the canvas Hero had long since scrawled the legend: 'Ilek-Vad.'

Unwashed, unshaven, he frowned again, turned and seated himself at a small desk. His mind was usually strangely fertile during its first waking moments. Rapidly he sketched upon a scrap of paper. Heavy hills quickly formed a background to his sketch, and in the foreground –

He grimaced at the hairy, insect-like dog-thing he had drawn, then crumpled the scrap into a ball and tossed it in his waste-basket. Wherever the inspiration for *that* came from, today he could well do without it! No, today was a day for walking in the city – or perhaps a trip out to the Firth of Forth Bridge, whose massive cantilever of almost four thousand feet never failed to fascinate him – or better still a day on the coast at Dunbar, where the seagulls called and the boys collected and sold empty, fist-sized sea urchin shells washed in on the tide. There was a place where he liked to sit on the rocks at the edge of the sea and look down into deep pools, where tiny fishes darted in deeps of waving weed.

No sooner had this thought occurred to him than another, far stranger vision came. In his mind's eye he stared down from Ilek-Vad's cliffs of green glass into waters where the finny and bearded Gnorri swam and, with their self-appointed and all-consuming industry, pursued the construction of intricate and utterly mazy labyrinths. This idea, coming so suddenly, startled David Hero. For *this* was surely inspiration! He had been commissioned to prepare a dust-jacket for an 'Epic of Submarine Science Fiction,' and the vision his mind had just conjured seemed near-perfect for his purpose: a scene of gentle, subaqueous beings going about their business among the caves of a fantastic seabed – and in the foreground, to one side of the main picture, weirdly-suited and armed intruders about to burst rapaciously upon the scene.

Excellent!

. . . But it could wait until later in the day, perhaps this evening. Right now Hero must wash and tidy up, make his breakfast and decide where the day's wanderings were to take him. Over eggs and bacon washed down with black coffee, he mentally reverted to his original choice: Edinburgh Castle. If ever a place were designed to create awe, wonder and inspiration in the eye of the beholder, surely this massive sky-climbing castle was that place. Yes, he would go there – and tonight he would start his sub-sea painting . . .

To the polyglot tourists who thronged the Royal Mile as Hero toiled up steeply slanting pavements past public houses and souvenir shops, he would not be too impressive a figure. In old jeans spotted with paint and

16

faded by sun and sea, and wearing his yellow hair long so that it lay on the shoulders of his dark, open-necked shirt, he might well be just another wastrel idling his time away in the hot summer days. And indeed, if such was the general suspicion, then it were not too seriously misplaced.

He was academically qualified, to be sure, but his tutors each and every one had found occasion to remark that he was 'much too much of a dreamer,' or 'given to flights of fancy totally removed from his studies.' The one field in which he felt truly at home – and in which he somehow managed to make his way in life – was painting, and this was really as much as he wanted to do. Oh, it would be nice to be rich, certainly, but not if that meant joining in the rat race. Since he was not without a degree of responsibility he could not be termed a dropout, but at the same time his ambitions were very limited.

His trouble was that he was a man born out of time, and perhaps out of place. He could well picture himself as a swashbuckling privateer on the Spanish Main, or an explorer of strange horizons on distant worlds – but never as an executive in some sprawling tower-block of offices on 20th Century Earth! Why, the very world felt alien to him, except in certain places. Edinburgh was one such place, with its fresh sea breezes and high-riding gulls, its castle, ancient monuments and general air of antiquity – for which reasons Hero could bear living here. And of course atmosphere was very important to his painting.

Eventually he found himself on the esplanade at the top of the Royal Mile, where he turned left out of the stream of tourists and went to lean on the old south wall. Beneath the wall the grass of the hillside fell swiftly away, merging into a rocky precipice which plunged down to a ribbonlike road that wound round

17

the castle rock and into the labyrinthine city.

High overhead the seagulls wheeled and cried in distant discord, and Hero found one with his binoculars, following the great circle of its effortless glide as it rose in the castle's thermal. For long moments the bird gained height, then deliberately turned out of the rising current of air and fell in great swoops towards the earth, down past the castle rock, down to where the circular structure of Granby Halls stood in the castle's shadow.

On a piece of waste ground beside the Halls stood a billboard, and there the gull came to rest, keenly scanning accumulated garbage dumped amongst weeds and wild ivy. Hero, following the gull's swoop, briefly scanned the billboard through his binoculars before he found the bird where it perched above the large, freshly-pasted poster. He found the bird . . . then frowned and lowered his glasses until the wording once more sprang into sharp relief. 'Dreams and their Meaning,' said the poster, and beneath this heading it displayed a legend in letters which were far smaller and less legible at this distance. Hero adjusted the binoculars and tried again, and after a moment's jiggling he managed to get the lower part of the poster into perspective.

DREAMS AND THEIR MEANING

The Extension of the Human Psyche into the Subconscious Realm of Dreams. Your Sleeping Fantasies explained in Layman's Language, by Scotland's Foremost Expert on the Hidden Worlds of the Mind!

There was more but the letters were much smaller and Hero was at a loss to further enlarge them and still retain a degree of clarity. Again he read the poster's more readily legible lettering and frowned, lowering the binoculars to let them hang on his chest. Dreams and their meanings? Foremost expert?

An expert on dreams . . .

Almost without knowning it, simply letting his feet take him, he left the esplanade, turned right off the Royal Mile and wended his way down into the city. In a little while he had found his way to the billboard and was able to read the rest of the poster's legend:

Tues, Wed, Thurs, this week. 8 p.m. – 9 p.m. – Professor Leonard Dingle (Psychology and Anthropology) talks on the fascinating subject of Man's secret desires, the dreams which motivate his every waking moment.

There was a little more in much the same vein, but Hero read no farther. Professor Leonard Dingle . . . There was something about that name. Something that rang bells of inquiry in the back of his memory. A bright vision of a bearded, burly face flashed in his mind's eye, then was gone. Did he know the man? But how could he know him?

And yet –

– It might be an interesting talk at that, and the dust-jacket painting could always wait until tomorrow. After all, what harm could there possibly be in attending a lecture?

The bells of inquiry in his mind turned to a distant, barely-heard clangor of alarm . . . but David Hero wasn't listening.

III
SECOND MEETING

The hall was hardly filled to capacity, anything but, and Hero suspected that things were not likely to improve. Since this was Tuesday and the first night of the lecture, it fully looked as though Prof. Leonard Dingle was in for a lean time of it. In the height of the tourist season, he must have been extremely fortunate to obtain the use of the hall in the first place – and surely this was the most dismal looking audience.

The hall was about one-third full of middle-aged ladies who looked like rejects from the bingo halls with nothing better to do; foreign tourists who fidgeted and chatted in diverse tongues, obviously having paid their entrance fee in error and wondering what time the main feature began; jean-clad, leather-jacketed roughnecks who appeared to be 'lying low' from someone or thing; and, in the rear row of seats, courting couples who plainly were not interested in anything the speaker or anyone else had to say.

Hero, arriving late, took all of this in as he entered the darkened hall to discover the lecture already underway. He found a seat three rows back from the front and having quietly made himself comfortable at last turned his attention to the speaker, 'Scotland's foremost expert on the hidden worlds of the mind.'

And here a paradox, for at one and the same time

Dingle was and was not exactly the figure Hero had expected! That is to say: while he was *not* the small, frail-looking, bespectacled and retiring chap his name and subject might suggest to the minds of most people, he very definitely *was* the burly, gangling figure Hero had glimpsed in his mind's eye while studying the poster. There were differences, however, and Hero found himself trying to pinpoint them as he studied the man where he stood behind a lectern, beneath a spotlight, talking into a microphone which amplified his voice only just sufficiently to make it audible at the back of the hall.

For one thing the speaker was clean shaven, which was inconsistent with Hero's pre-cognitive glimpse, and for another he was far more articulate than Hero had pictured him. This of course was only to be expected in a man who delivered talks and lectures, and yet somehow Hero had not expected it. The voice was deep and fairly impressive, as he had somehow guessed it would be, and marred by an irritating cough or the suspicion of one, which also seemed to fit the artist's preconception. And yet, for all Dingle's aggressive-seeming stance and gangling appearance (and despite the fact that one side of his face looked to be familiarly scarred), still he seemed much too much the scholar and gentleman to truly represent Hero's previous – knowledge? – of him. Again the artist found himself wondering: did he *know* the man? And if so, where had he met him before?

But at last the professor's message was getting through to Hero, and despite his consuming curiosity about the man *himself* he became gradually drawn in by the speaker's subject and gripped by his words. For certainly Dingle knew his stuff.

'Most people at some time or other have been puzzled by dreams,' the professor was saying. 'Dreams are often thought of as mere curiosities, occasionally prophecies, omens and sometimes parapsychological experiences. Periodicals may today be purchased which purport to "translate" dreams into forms which have commonplace or at least everyday meanings and applications.

'But what do dreams *really* mean? What are they all about? Was Sigmund Freud right? Can dreams be explained away simply by calling them "primary processes" of the mind? Are they indeed the "royal road to the unconscious mind," disguised expressions of otherwise suppressed urges?

'Modern thinking, with some aid from "hardware" science as opposed to the science of psychology, would seem to show that Freud's conclusions are not altogether complete. A recent theory has it that our minds are computers, which require regular "clearing." That is, the removal of superfluous programming. Dreams perform the clearing, getting rid of accumulated and unwanted experiences, the mental garbage of conscious existence. Pretty clever . . .

'But is that it? Is that all? Is that *really* all there is to it?

'I for one don't think so. There are – anomalies. Big ones!

'For instance: how may we explain Kekulé's dream of the benzene ring, wherein a complicated molecular structure which had baffled many scientists was suddenly made clear to the dreamer? Astonishing!

'Or could it be that dreams serve the purpose of solving problems which are too difficult for a merely conscious, cluttered mind to comprehend? H.P. Lovecraft, a writer of horror stories who was anything but prolific, actually dreamed entire stories – almost as if his dreaming mind were trying to solve his waking problems! Of these dream-tales, several were published and are fairly good examples of their genre.

'And so in Lovecraft's case we see that something solid actually came out of the allegedly insubstantial world of his dreams. I ask myself: could that world really be so insubstantial? And if dreams are so ethereal, what of Gerhard Schrach's statement on the insubstantiality of so-called solids? His own dreams, you may remember, were so "real" that he was ever at a loss to know which world was the more vital, the waking world or the world of dreams.

'Once, in Vienna, I was fortunate enough to meet and talk at some length with Schrach about some of his "experiences" in those subconscious realms of his mind which he termed "the dreamlands." For it seemed to Schrach that those brief periods of our sleeping lives which the great majority of people term "dreams" were not dreams at all as he understood the term but merely reflections of the waking world impinging on the surface of the subconscious mind during its shallower sleep-times. To discover the real dreamlands, Schrach said, one must go much deeper.

'For Gerhard Schrach's dreaming took the form of a separate and solid existence which he believed lies at the roots of Man's subconscious. Not merely *his own* subconscious, you understand, but Man's. He believed that if only we knew how, then all of us might explore those selfsame worlds of wonder! But even so, it would be an exceptionally rare dreamer indeed who could bring back even a fragmentary recollection to the waking world.

'As I have said, he was just such a man, and I was so impressed with the *depth* and *detail* of what he told me he had dreamed that I found myself actually carried along by his recounting of his adventures in those dreamlands; by tales and descriptions of dreamland's customs, peoples, rivers and hills and cities.

24

'Yes, it actually seemed to me as I listened to Schrach that I, too, had known such rivers as the Skai and the Tross, such cities as Ulthar, Celephais and Ilek-Vad . . .'

Ulthar, Celephais and Ilek-Vad!

Hero jerked upright in his seat and his hair felt full of some weird energy, an electrical prickling which crawled across his scalp and down his neck to solicit a response from his suddenly charged skin, covering him in shuddery goose-pimples. Ulthar, Celephais and Ilek-Vad!

What in the name of everything holy . . .?

This man on the stage in the haze of his spotlight – this familiar stranger Hero could not possibly but *did* somehow recognize – was talking of the subconscious world of another man's dreaming imagination; and yet David Hero, too, had somewhere known those fabled names and places before. Why, when his own imagination was working at its strongest, he even *painted* them!

Hero heard no more but stumbled to his feet. He was utterly shaken, numb, as he made his way to the foyer, and from there to the wings of the stage, where he waited in a sort of euphoric stupor for Dingle to finish his monologue. He heard little of what remained of the professor's talk, however, for his head was humming with winds of mystery, his mind's eye full of half-seen visions that could not quite be brought into perspective. He stood, he knew, on the threshold of something quite momentous, something unique.

And always he kept asking himself: how could this be? Had he heard a-right? Did he and Gerhard Schrach – yes, and perhaps Leonard Dingle, too – share in part a mutual dream-world which, upon awakening, they left behind except for the occasional tantalizing glimpse or vision? Or had Schrach perhaps written of the lands of his dreaming; and then without knowing it, had Hero somewhere long ago read his work and remembered it, so that the names of certain dream-places and something of their descriptions had stuck in his head?

There was that possibility, of course, but Hero did not believe that was the answer. For even now, as he impatiently waited for the professor to finish, misted visions of incredible lands beyond the boundaries of the conscious world kept flashing across his mind, half-glimpsed and transient, and yet real, he knew . . .

At last it was over and the lights went up on a hall containing less than half of its original number. The roughnecks had departed to face whichever fate pursued or waited for them; the foreign tourists had long since discovered their error and taken their leave of the place; and at last the small core of the audience got wearily to its feet and made to pass out into the city, where by now the twilight of evening would be silently settling.

Hero met Dingle in the wings with: 'Sir, my name is David Hero, and –'

'Hero, d'you say?' Dingle rumbled, tucking his crammed briefcase under one great arm. He looked at Hero closely and his forehead wrinkled in a frown. 'We've met somewhere before, eh?'

Hero's heart gave a mighty lurch. 'I . . . I don't think so,' he answered; then quickly added: 'Yes I do – but I don't know where. I was hoping you . . .?' And he paused, not quite knowing how to explain his presence here in the wings.

'Hero, eh? Hmm,' the professor rumbled. 'The name rings a bell. You're from the south, yes?'

'The north-east coast of England, yes,' Hero nodded.

'I'm from the Midlands myself. Seems unlikely we'd ever come together. What brings you to Edinburgh?'

'I live here – now,' Hero explained. 'I'm an artist, when I'm anything at all. As to why I'm here: the city has an atmosphere like no other. It's like a stepping-off place to –' he shrugged.

'I know what you mean,' Dingle rumbled, and coughed a little as a shadow of pain crossed his face. 'You'll excuse my cough,' he hastily said. 'That's *my* main reason for being here. I've lived here for some time, but I go even farther up north whenever I can. It's good clean air up there. Scotland: the last bastion of civilized, air-breathing man. At least in this world . . .'

'In this world?' Once again Hero felt the weird tingling of his scalp. 'What other world is there?'

'Ah!' Dingle smiled. 'Well now, that's a secret between me and myself.' He picked up a poster or two, threw a coat over his arm and prepared to leave the Halls. 'Were you part of the, er, "audience," Mr Hero?' He grinned ruefully.

'For a while,' the other nodded. Then, unable to hold himself back any longer, he blurted: 'Is that what you meant by another world? The world of Ilek-Vad and Dylath-Leen?'

'Dylath –' the other gasped, dropping his briefcase so that it burst open and scattered its contents on the floor. 'I made no mention of –'

'But you know it, don't you? You've heard of it before?'

Dumbly the professor nodded, then grasped Hero by the shoulders. In a half-whisper he said: 'And Oriab in the Southern Sea?'

'With its coastal, capital city, Baharna. And Hatheg-Kla in the stony desert?'

27

'Which Atal the Ancient climbed in his youth –'

'– From which only he returned while Barzai the Unwise remained behind!'

After a long moment the professor said: 'They come and go, these visions, and when they're gone I hunger after them.' His grip tightened on Hero's shoulders. 'You wouldn't be having a little practical joke at my expense?'

Hero shook his head. 'No. Here in Edinburgh, this is where it's strongest for me. It was the same in Durham City, and Whitby on the coast, but not so strong. Listen, I've got paintings at home: of Ilek-Vad and Dylath-Leen. Yes, and others.'

'It's so hard to believe . . .' Dingle began. Then: he fixed Hero with suddenly sharp eyes and said, 'What do you know of . . . of Ulthar?' And Hero knew that this was the final test.

Suddenly, from nowhere, the answer came; a memory from limitless depths of dream. 'It lies beyond the Skai. In Ulthar, no man may kill a cat!'

Dingle's hands fell from Hero's shoulders and he slumped wearily against a wall. 'Not even Gerhard Schrach remembered that,' he finally said. 'You have pictures, you say? Where do you live?'

'Not far. In the Dalkeith Road.'

'I'm in Musselburgh. May I offer you a lift home? Perhaps I could see your paintings . . .?'

In Dingle's tiny Fiat, whose pistons clattered as the professor raced it through the streets, its headlights probing the cobbled ways ahead, the two sat hunched in mutual astonishment. Neither one quite believed the evidence of his own senses; and occasionally, as ideas came, they would put each other to the test:

'They say that Thalarion is demon-cursed –' Hero began.

'Where the Eidolon Lathi rules a monstrous hive of

horror,' Dingle finished it for him, without quite realizing where such esoteric knowledge came from.

'And what lies beyond the Basalt Pillars of the West, I wonder?'

'Splendid Cathuria, some say. But what of Zoogs and Ghasts?'

'And Gaunts and spider-hounds . . .'

With a mutual gasp they turned to one another. And all the superficiality of the waking world melted away in an instant of time. '*Eldin!*' Hero croaked. 'Eldin the Wanderer – Prof. L. Dingle!'

'Hero!' cried the other. 'David Hero, no less, who saved my life in the northern uplands!'

At that very moment the professor's tiny car shot through a light which was red. The blaring of a massive horn, the screech and *hiss* of powerful air-brakes and the vastly glaring lights of an articulated juggernaut seemed suddenly to fill the whole world.

There followed rushing, headlong motion, tearing pain and a hungry black vortex that sucked both men down, down, down to worlds of wonder as old as the dreaming Mind of Mankind . . .

PART TWO

I

EBRAIM BORAK

Two big men they were that walked their greak yaks out of the river mists that night, wandering dreamers long departed the teeming cities of the waking world to seek their fortunes in dreamland's coastal towns and villages. But despite the fact that these were men of the waking world (who have always been, in physical stature, greater than those of dreamland) their bigness lay not alone in powerful muscles and towering frames of flesh. No, for in the years of their companionship they had also acquired a certain stature in the art of thievery.

As to the passage of time:

Since that early morning when, against his will and better judgment, David Hero had descended the seven hundred steps to pass through the Gate of Deeper Slumber – and later to find Eldin where he lodged for a day or two at a village inn – a great many mornings had seemed to pass and time had become a confusion; which is usually the way of it with dreams.

For as any dreamer can testify, dream-time passes very strangely – where entire adventures may take place in a single hour, and an hour itself lengthen to a week – so that a year in dreamland might easily pass between the closing of one's eyes and their opening to a single morning's sun in the waking world. But even so, Eldin and Hero had seemed to wander an inordinately long time; and surely one or the other, or both, ought by now to have returned through the thin veil of sleep to the world of their conscious beings?

They had not done so, however, and since neither one of them could remember the circumstances which had occasioned their meeting in the waking world – or the terrible accident which returned them once again to the dreamland where now they had come together – they had long since given up trying to fathom the riddle of it. They were now, to all intents and purposes, inhabitants of dream; though to dreamland's genuine citizens they would always be 'men of the waking world.'

And of course they were the two dreamers who came down into Theelys: David Hero and Eldin the Wanderer, grown closer now than brothers and questing after – what? But questing, anyway.

The ferryman who brought them across the mouth of the Tross had known something of them, but had said nothing. And for all that they towered over him, still they had paid for his services and made no trouble for him. Others in dreamland had not been so lucky where these two were concerned, the ferryman knew, but he also knew that their reputation was not a bad one. They were thieves and known for their brawling, true, but they stole only from those whose fortunes were great (and usually ill-gotten) and they brawled with those of their own kind, in which fighting seemed instinct. Outlaws they might be – but not yet outcasts.

In the passing years Eldin had grown somewhat quick to anger, but his loyalty to his companion remained unswervable. Scarfaced, black-browed and gangling like an ape, now he sucked in the river mists and gritted his teeth, straining to control the red coughing that threatened constantly to explode deep in his lungs, a condition that worsened as the seasons waxed and waned.

Hero, on the other hand, had seemed to profit from his long immersion in dream. Tall, rangily muscled, and blond as his waking self – blue of eye and fleet of foot, bursting with easy laughter and, in a tight corner, wizard-master of a flickering snake's tongue in the shape of a curved blade of jungled Kled – he loved songs, a good fight, and sometimes girls. He was younger by a good fifteen years than his companion and clad in brown as compared with the other's night black, but the lands of dream have often known stranger comrades. At least the two were of the same basic mind and shared the same wild wanderlust. Now that wanderlust had brought them south and east, and having crossed the River Tross by ferry, at last they were come down into Theelys.

Of money they had very little – sufficient only for a day or two's bed and board, and perhaps a little extra for a wineskin or so if they carefully avoided the gaming-houses – so that they were sharp-eyed and eager for easy pickings. Thus, in the Street of Rats, at that hour when torches are lit against the dank mists of the Tross, they stabled their yaks and put up at the tavern of Hymat Zorathin. There they tossed their few belongings into a tiny room with a pair of even tinier bunks before elbowing their way into the aleroom and securing a corner table. With their backs safely to the baked brick wall and a wineskin between them – in the warm, noisy, smoky atmosphere of the low-ceilinged tavern – they felt at ease and began to cast about with practiced eyes to see what they might see.

And they were not the only ones in Hymat Zorathin's house with hard bright eyes that night. No, indeed; for in the shadows across the room, where the red and yellow flickering of the torches barely reached, a hooded figure stood silently apart from the tavern's boozier customers and regarded the new-comers thoughtfully through orbs that were sly beneath high-pointed brows.

This was Ebraim Borak, outcast of the Ossaran Steppes many hundreds of miles to the east, a man who employed his keen wits and skeptic's knowledge of human nature to live a life of comparative luxury. In the waking world he had been an arms manufac-turer, asleep and dreaming when a barrel of his own explosive had stranded him forever in the dreamlands.

His house was in a lordly quarter of the city, wherein he kept a handful of beautiful black slavegirls of Parg and a eunuch manservant or two, but his presence in this lowly tavern was not unusual. Often in such places he found men and women whose vari-ous talents were suited to his own equally varied needs. And his interest in the two dreamers sprang chiefly from the fact that he recognized their hooded, hungry peering, knew their precarious position, their almost penniless condition . . . which in turn ought to make them ideal tools for a certain scheme of his.

Some years ago the wizard Nyrass of Theelys, whose walled and high-turreted castle loomed on the outskirts of the city, had promised Borak great riches, wealth almost beyond reckoning, if he could only devise a means of stealing (the wizard had called it 'acquiring') a certain magical wand. This wand was a prized possession of an ancient and extremely wicked priest of the dark 'God' Yibb-Tstll, who tended his duties at the feet of the monstrous stone idol of that god in a dark temple high in the Great Bleak Moun-tains (which range of mountains certain authorities believe to be the foothills of that ultimate plateau, Kadath in the Cold Waste).

The wizard Nyrass, a good man despite his various thaumaturgies and magical machinations, had openly warned Borak that the dangers attendant upon any attempted larceny of the wand would be great indeed. To begin with, Yibb-Tstll's priest was a worshipper of the terrible demon gods who seeped down with Cthulhu from the stars when the Earth was an inchoate infant and dreamland still undreamed. And he was rumoured to wield weird powers, for through the wand he controlled an alien energy which could shrivel men to bones like the blast of a mighty furnace or the heat in the heart of a rumbling volcano.

And then there was the stone idol, which, if the right runes were invoked and certain other sigils applied, could take on a semblance of life and walk abroad even as Yibb-Tstll himself. And Yibb-Tstll was grim indeed, tainted with all the vile lusts of the terrible demon gods, of which he was one. Against dangers such as these the dizzy mountains and the often perpendicular climbs necessary to reach the temple of the god were as nothing, neither those nor the snow-leopards or even the night-gaunts which were believed to inhabit the caves of the upper crags.

And so Ebraim Borak knew that the road to Yibb-Tstll's dark temple was fraught with danger, and the stealing of his priest's wand even more so, for which reasons (and for one other) he was not greatly surprised that of the wanderers he had sent to steal and bring back the wand – eight men so far; a group of four, a pair, and two other lone adventurers – no single word had since been heard.

Doubtless they had followed the Tross to its source somewhere in the mountainous heights, where the massively monolithic Keeps of the First Ones were known to stand featureless and fearsome, vast blocks of stone as high as the hills, pitted by centuries of rain and ice and lightnings. Eight prospective pillagers, aye – but not a man of them had ever returned! Borak knew why this was so; indeed, he knew much more than the good wizard Nyrass suspected.

For unbeknown to Nyrass, Borak had found a way to contact the wizard-priest of the mountains, discovering him to be a cousin of Nyrass, one Thinistor Udd. Udd in turn had engaged Borak's services, offering him two thousand tonds for each man he could send him; but he must never send more than four at any one time. Borak did not question the sinister wizard's requirements; his greed put aside all need for questions and there was no such thing as 'ethics' in his business. Since Nyrass also paid Borak's 'expenses,' and since no one ever returned from his fool's errand to claim the reward, the Ossaran was in an enviable position – for a man without scruples. And if ever some fool should win Thinistor Udd's wand: well, he could always be disposed of, and then Borak would lay claim to the aforementioned riches promised him by the wizard Nyrass.

Thus was Ebraim Borak a web for the spider Thinistor Udd, and the poor fools who fell in with his plans mere flies for that wizard's larder. And now, here, if he gauged his men aright, benevolent fates had sent him two more adventurous souls whose paths he could doubtless turn to the north. A few pieces of gold and a promise or two . . . there were those in certain quarters of Theelys would gut their grandmothers for a half-tond. Such men were not, however, suited to the Ossaran's needs. These wanderers from the waking world, on the other hand . . .

*   *   *

'That man,' Eldin softly growled, almost impercept-
ibly nodding in the direction of a staggering, drunken
Kledan slaver whose brawny black arms were banded
with gold, 'ought not to go home alone. Why, in his
condition and with the mist so thick outside, almost
anything might befall him on his way back to the
black quarter. Eh?' He took his eyes from the
lurching, ale-slopping Kledan, indelicately squirted a
burst of wine into his mouth, and laughingly slapped
his younger companion on the back, as if he had just
told some remarkably good joke.

David Hero grinned back at his friend, shook a
long yellow lock of hair out of wide blue eyes, and
answered: 'Aye, there are many dark alleys between
him and his bed. Some high-spirited lad might easily
bump into him in the dark and inadvertently knock
him off his feet. It would be the ruin of those baggy
silk pants . . .'

The Kledan swayed wildly and half fell, then somehow managed to straighten up. He headed unevenly
for the exit, eyes glazed, arms adangle, pushing
smaller men out of his way as he went. When his head
struck against an especially low beam he reeled and
cursed aloud in guttural jungle-born accents, finally
teetering through a hanging curtain of beads into the
narrow passage that led out onto the Street of Rats.

Eldin was half-way to his feet when a well-
manicured but firm hand fell upon his shoulder,
pushing him back. Unseen in the momentary
diversion caused by the Kledan's ungainly exit,
Ebraim Borak had made his way over to the
dreamers. Now he loomed over them, too tall for a
man born of the dreamlands but proud-featured as
the race which had first adopted him.

'Easy, my friend,' Borak murmured, smiling from
beneath the hood of his rich red robe. 'There are

easier ways to make a living, I assure you – and any-way, the foggy air will quickly sober him up. You'd not get away with it, for they'd notice you leaving hot on his trail. The jails of the city are full of would-be pickpockets, sharpers and cutthroats.' He seated himself easily between the dreamers and clapped his hands, ordering a skin of the tavern's finest wine.

'We wouldn't have cut his throat,' Hero protested in lowered tones. 'Merely tapped him on the head, that's all.'

'Aye,' Eldin agreed, 'and in the morning he'd surely thank us for a good night's sleep – and any-way, those golden bangles of his must weigh a ton. They're like to break the poor fellow's arms!'

'Then you admit you were up to no good?'

'Little point in denying it,' answered Eldin, stifling a painful cough, 'since you've obviously travelled that road yourself. And would you tell on us?'

'Not I,' answered the Ossaran, holding up his hands in denial. 'Indeed, and as you correctly deduce, if times were harder – and they often have been – I might myself entertain just such wild designs. No, I'm here to make you an offer, not to deliver you into the hands of the city's jailers. Besides, I've little enough time for the law. My own reputation reaches far back into the past and is less than . . . spotless? And that, gentlemen,' he hurriedly went on, 'is not meant as a slur on your own characters, I assure you.'

'In which case,' rumbled Eldin bringing into view from beneath the table a curving dagger whose blade reflected the poor light glintingly, 'there's no require-ment for this!' He slipped the weapon into its scab-bard at his belt.

Borak's eye narrowed beneath the hood of his cloak in grudging, wary admiration as he gazed at the burly dreamer. 'Well then,' he eventually continued, 'before we get down to business: how are you named, you two, and what's your trade? – other than rolling drunks, that is.'

'Rolling drunks is part of it,' Hero nodded, frowning. 'When you have nothing and you've reached nowhere you start again – at the bottom. At the moment we're thieves, that's all.'

His larger companion grunted in agreement. 'There's more money in thieving than trading in dreamland's wares,' he said, 'and the work is easier – until you're caught. We haven't been caught yet, and we don't intend to be. As for our names: this is David Hero and I'm Eldin the Wanderer, and we've roved and robbed half across dreamland, always in search of –'

'In search of?' Borak prompted him. 'Of what? Wealth, a good woman, a place to settle, adventure, life . . . death?'

'All of those things,' Eldin snarled, suddenly impatient and curiously peeved by Borak's questioning. 'What more is there?' He coughed again, an expression of pain momentarily twisting his already unlovely features.

Borak shrugged, then answered shrewdly: 'What more? An easy life – while you still have one to live!' He turned to Hero. 'Wouldn't you agree?'

'Easy living would be nice I suppose, for a while,' came the answer. 'But there's more, there must be. More than wealth and property, more than a pretty girl and a warm hearth to park your boots on. Adventure? – maybe that's it. There's always a hill behind the next one, always an uncharted island somewhere, a scent you never smelled before, a taste you never tasted . . .'

Borak lifted an eyebrow in surprise. 'Are you a poet then, dreamer, as well as a thief?' He turned his gaze

41

once more upon the heavier man. 'And yet your friend here seems just the opposite. You make a strange pair.'

'I'm a bit of a poet, that's true,' agreed Hero, 'but don't misjudge Eldin. His nature was once pretty much like mine. Now –' he shrugged. 'Don't they say that opposites attract? Anyway, we understand each other – and we'd understand you better, too, if you'd only get to the point.'

'Aye,' the Ossaran agreed, 'enough useless chattering.' He stirred himself, took out a leather pouch, emptied its contents carefully onto the table. One hundred triangular tonds, the principal coinage of the south-east, lay golden and gleaming in the tavern's smoky light. Silence fell over the room in an instant and every eye glitteringly reflected the gold.

Softly humming an olden tune of the steppes to himself, Borak deliberately divided the heap into two equal piles, one for David Hero and the other for Eldin the Wanderer. The hand of the older dreamer was touching his pile when the younger's trapped his wrist. Their bright eyes met across the table questioningly, then turned to stare at Ebraim Borak.

'We could live like kings for a three-month!' Hero murmured. 'But what do you want of us for your money?'

'He wants someone murdered,' Eldin grunted. 'Isn't it obvious?'

Ebraim Borak shook his head and smiled. 'No, I'm not hiring assassins,' he assured them. 'Not tonight. If murder was what I wanted I could get it cheaper than this, I promise you. All I want is your attention, to know that you'll hear me out. The money is payment in advance for that alone. Then, if I can interest you in my proposition –' he formed his next words carefully in a voice little louder than a whisper: 'Five hundred tonds each as a retainer – ten thousand when the job is done!'

'Ten thousand tonds,' Hero whistled softly. 'That's five thousand each!'

'No, no, my young friend,' Borak quickly corrected him. 'You misunderstand me. I meant ten thousand . . . *each*!'

After a period of stunned silence, Eldin grunted and scooped up his pile of money. 'Oh, we'll listen,' he nodded his head emphatically. 'You may be sure of that!'

'Aye,' agreed the younger man, letting his pile of tonds lie. 'But listening is a thirsty game, eh? So – taverner!' he called out. 'Another skin, if you please. No, better make it three – and some meat to soak it up!'

II
OF OMENS AND NIGHT-GAUNTS

In the foothills of the Great Bleak Mountains, two hundred miles north of Theelys and three weeks later, as evening settled in and a pair of great kites soared on high, eyes sharp for unwary rabbits, the dreamers added their own lengthening shadows to the greater darkness beneath an overhanging outcrop of rock and spread their blankets in preparation for the night.

They freed their single yak from the trappings of its light-framed travois and tethered it where the new spring grass stood green in the fading light. It was not an especially cold night but Hero threw a blanket over the yak anyway. The animal was his, Eldin's mount having fallen foul of a rock viper's bite five days gone; and since then the dreamers had walked while the animal pulled the weight of their various necessaries upon its rough but sturdily constructed travois.

This last day had been harder than the rest of the journey, for they had climbed constantly up through the steep foothills until now, with the night, they were come at last to the feet of the Great Bleak Mountains. Tomorrow would be that much harder.

So, to fortify themselves in advance, they roasted a rabbit over a wood fire and brewed up a pan of sweet tea from the Ossaran Steppes, talking in low, weary tones while the silence of night deepened and the stars began to show beyond the lip of the overhang. As they rested on their blankets a shooting-star raced down across blue-black heavens of dreamland.

'An omen,' murmured Hero.

His companion merely grunted. 'A star,' he answered after a while. 'Only a star, falling out of the sky.'

'An omen nonetheless,' the younger man insisted.

Again Eldin grunted. 'As you wish,' he said. Then: 'A good omen – or a bad one?'

A shrug in the fire-flickered darkness. 'Who can say?'

Disgruntled, the older man snarled: 'Then why worry about it?'

'Oh, omens are worth watching out for.'

'Huh!'

A moment or two later, as Hero settled himself down and pulled his blanket up to his chin, Eldin began to cough. Long and wrackingly he coughed, and when it seemed that he might never stop his companion stirred himself to ask: 'Are you all right, old friend?'

The coughing subsided. Eldin spat onto a rock beside the guttering fire. He dabbled his finger in the spittle and showed it to Hero. In the dying light from the fire the younger man saw traces of frothy red.

'Now that's what I call an omen,' said Eldin, and he laughed low and bitterly.

At noon the next day they set the yak free and with a slap on its rump Hero said his farewell to the animal. It trotted away back down the slope that had steepened all through the morning, only pausing at a defile to turn its head and look back. Then it snorted, tossed its head once and was gone, around a rocky spur and lost from sight.

From now on it was to be a climb, not sheer yet by any means but steep by any man's judgment. High overhead were the snows, melting on the lower slopes but still heavy in the peaks of this section of the Great Bleak Range. Icy water rushed down from above, a wide waterfall in the main, for way up ahead in the peaks the Tross had its secret source.

Midway through the afternoon they took a break, ate a meal, drank tea and talked as they had talked a hundred times since leaving Theelys after a week's debauchery at Ebraim Borak's expense. Of money they still had plenty, were rich by any dreamer's standards, but Borak had promised much more. This was the topic of their conversation:

'I can understand the Ossaran paying good money for this mysterious wand – which must after all be worth many times what he's willing to pay for it – but how can he be sure we'll ever bring the thing back to him?' Eldin squinted at his younger companion, scowling through the smoke of their small fire.

'Where else could we sell it – and who could afford to buy?' Hero answered realistically. 'A wand, that's all it is – a stick or a rod – and you can't eat wands, you know. And damned if I'd know how to use it. But when we take it back to Ebraim Borak, then we'll have money for life. And we *do* know how to use that! Oh, Borak's sure enough we'll deliver it . . . *if* we ever get it.'

'Maybe,' the other dreamer grunted, 'but there are plenty of rich Lords in dreamland. If we were dishonest men' (at which Hero chuckled), 'we might easily –'

'Easily what, Eldin? Sell Borak out to some rich Lord? Do you know what that rich Lord would do?

47

Throw us in a cell and have us tortured until we told where we got the wand, that's what! And then, when we told? He'd have us put to death! How do you suppose these rich Lords got to be so rich?'

'Yes, I know, I know,' Eldin rumbled, 'but they're not all bad. Still, there's that about this quest that worries me sorely. I mean, if the job's to be so easy, why didn't Borak come and do it himself?'

'What? A cultured city gent up here in the heights of the Great Bleak Mountains? Battling the elements and venturing along unknown ways and all –'

'All rubbish!' Eldin finished it for him. 'An Ossaran, "cultured," indeed!'

'Spoken like a true expert,' Hero laughed derisively. 'And what, pray, would a bloodstained thief of a marooned dreamer know about culture?'

'Huh! I've a suspicion I'm a pretty smart fellow in the waking world,' Eldin muttered.

'Oh? Well I wouldn't know. But anyway, I think your questions are all easily enough answered. No, this job Borak's given us will *not* be the simple thing he made it sound. And yes, there are certain dangers other than those he mentioned. If there weren't, someone else would have stolen the wand long ago.'

'But that's just it! What dangers can there be? A few cliffs to climb and maybe a gaunt or two to wing us away in the dead of night? A handful of snow-leopards and a doddery old priest guarding a stone god in a cavern temple? To dreamers such as you and I, surely these are mere irritations?'

Hero nodded. 'Aye, so it would seem. And yet I'm sure that it won't be at all easy. And don't scoff at such things as night-gaunts. In Celephaïs I talked to a prospector who once had a brush with gaunts when he was climbing in the Heights of Lerion. He was panning streams for gold at the time.

'Well, he camped one night in a saddle between two ridges – and woke to find himself already aloft, in a great flapping of leathery wings! Two of them had him between them, and they were heading north. He put up such a fight in the dark that he soon made them lose height, and before very long he felt his feet dragging over solid ground.

'He broke free from one of the gaunts, got out his knife and stabbed the other, wounding it. He was winded when the injured creature fell with him, but not much. He jumped up and cut the head off the gaunt, then hid in a cave till morning. When it was light he went out and found the carcass of the one he'd killed – its carcass and its head . . .' Hero paused to pull a sour face.

'Go on,' again his friend prompted him. 'And?'

'There was no face on the gaunt's head!'

Eldin grunted and nodded. 'I've heard that said of gaunts before: that they have no faces.' He shuddered involuntarily.

'Well,' Hero continued presently, 'finally the old prospector got down out of the hills and made his way back to Celephais. He'd been away such a long time that his wife gave him hell!'

Eldin grunted again. 'Huh! Precipices and snow-leopards – old priests and secret temples – bitter-cold mountain heights and faceless night-gaunts . . . what in the names of all the gods are we in this for, David?'

'Money, old friend,' the other reminded him, pouring out two more tiny cups of tea with one hand and buttoning his brown jacket more warmly about his throat with the other. 'We're only here for the money . . .'

III
THE CAVE IN THE MOUNTAINS

Three days and nights later – three days of finger-skinning, back-breaking, nerve-wrenching climbing and clawing up precipitous walls of crumbling rock; three nights of camping-down on narrow, bitter, blustily-exposed ledges overhanging thousands of feet of empty air – then . . .

. . . Wearily hauling himself up onto what seemed like the thousandth crest of the thousandth ridge a few paces in front of Eldin, Hero gave a low, breathless whistle and paused to stand and stare, mouth agape and sucking hungrily at air, in awe of the titanic monolith which now reared its monstrous, featureless cube before him. One of the Keeps of the First Ones: its foot dimly shadowed and wreathed in late morning mist, its towering summit stained, mottled and weathered by the passage of nameless centuries.

The vast stone block was set back from the sheer, freshly-conquered face, looming in the final fold of mountain that went up, white-crested, to the ultimate ridge of snow. Neither door nor window showed, nor indeed any evidence at all to show that the structure had ever known or been capable of knowing habitation of any sort, and yet patently it was not a natural feature; it had been fashioned by intelligent beings.

Hero stared a moment longer; then his eyes went to the distance that separated him from the base of the massive keep. His jaw dropped farther yet when he saw that the foot of the keep, far from being close at hand, was at least a quarter-mile away from him across this rocky and snow-patched penultimate plateau. Suddenly the keep seemed to loom even larger in the eye of his imagination, and he wondered at the nature of its builders, starting violently when Eldin's heavy hand fell upon his shoulder.

'Nervous, my friend?' inquired the latecomer in his deep bass rumble.

'Aye,' Hero answered; then, catching sight of a white, moving blur in the corner of his eye: 'And rightly so! *Guard yourself, brother*!'

Out of a large patch of snow that dazzled with its myriad reflections of sun-sparkle, the white blur – springing apart and forming two blurs, two pure white, snarling, furious snow-leopards – shot straight at them. The creatures, each as heavy as a small man, covered the distance between in the merest twinkling of an eye, but that was as much time as the wandering dreamers needed.

As the first beast sprang at Hero he fell to his knees, his curved blade leaving its scabbard with a steely whisper, slicing upward to slit open the great cat's belly in one clean, deep, killing cut. Behind Hero, the snow-leopard hit the ground, scrabbling yowlingly for a split second in its own steaming entrails, then skidded in a white and scarlet blob over the lip and into space.

Springing to his feet the lithe dreamer whirled – in time to see Eldin behead the second cat with a single swing of his long, straight blade. This was an act of mercy, for with a blow unseen by his companion, the gruff Wanderer had already almost sliced the beast in two parts. Now, the short hairs of his neck a-bristle, Eldin poked at the cat's carcass with the tip of his sword.

'Did that one of yours wear a collar?' he asked of the younger man.

'I can't honestly say that I looked,' Hero replied.

'Well, this one wears a collar.'

'So I see. A welcoming committee, d'you think?'

Eldin shook his head negatively. 'No. See over there?' He pointed to where the snow showed pink, where a broken shape lay huddled in death. 'They'd caught a goat when we disturbed them. They'd been let out to find food for themselves, that's all.'

'Huh!' grunted Hero. 'Well, they'll not be going home again, that's for sure . . .'

'Home?' repeated the other, making it a question, his voice a low rumble as he shielded his eyes against snow-glare and scanned the false summit with its looming, featureless keep. 'Home, aye – and where might home be, I wonder? – and who the master there, that runs hounds such as these?'

'What did the Ossaran tell us?' Hero inquired, and immediately answered himself, intoning: ' ' 'Behind the keep, where the mountain overhangs, there in a deep cave –'' '

' ''That's where you'll find Yibb-Tstll's temple, and the idol of stone fashioned in his image – and Thinistor Udd and his magic wand,'' ' Eldin finished it. 'Well then, do we approach head on, all caution to the wind? Or should we sidle around the great keep and follow the foot of this last rise to the cave's entrance? Or perhaps –'

'We should wait for evening,' added Hero, equally adept at interrupting. 'That small and extremely comfortable-looking cave we passed a minute ago on the way up will suit us ideally. Snow-leopard steaks, hot tea, an afternoon's sleep all snug in our blankets – and after that we'll feel more like facing whatever's ahead. Come evening we'll get into the shadow of the keep and from then on trust to luck and a pair of bright blades!'

Eldin approvingly patted his companion on the shoulder. 'You're a clever lad,' he growled, 'for all that you still use your waking world-name. Right, you go on back down and I'll lower this poor dead pussy-cat down to you.' He rubbed his great hands briskly together and smacked his lips. 'By Koth's awful sign, I can taste those steaks already!'

Eldin's painfully wracking cough woke Hero up. The older dreamer sat in his blanket, holding his chest, rocking to and fro and coughing fit to die.

'Which,' (thought Hero), 'sooner or later, is exactly what he'll do!' But to his sick colleague, out loud, he said: 'There can't be a deal wrong with lungs as noisy as those of yours, old friend.'

'Huh!' The other's spasms finally subsided. 'And who was it said that the mountain air was sure to do me good? Well, you're not often right, David, but you're wrong again!'

Laughing, Hero stretched, shrugged out of his blanket and came to his feet, careful to avoid cracking his head against the low ceiling. The fire – built of large sticks from the violated nest of a spotted eagle and fortified with dried goat dung – had long since burned itself out and shadows were sharply etched in the cave. Outside, evening had crept over dreamland and soon the first stars would begin to show them-selves in the darkening sky.

Leaving all of their necessaries in the cave, the adventurers climbed up again to the vast and now shadowy shelf in silence. Something of a wind blew in their faces as they emerged onto the plateau-like surface, a strangely warm wind that sprang from its unknown source beyond the mountains. The dreamers had already formed the opinion that the old legends and rumours were false and that these mountains were not Kadath's foothills, and now this wind in their faces seemed fully to confirm their belief. For Kadath lay in the Cold Waste, and this wind from the north was a warm one.

But the wind soon died away and despite the fact that they were well wrapped, soon the bitter cold of the evening mountains began to gnaw into them, particularly when they passed into the shade of the towering Keep of the First Ones. Both of them shuddered a little then, and drew their clothing more tightly about themselves.

Moving faster now they passed round the foot of the keep, skirting jagged stones and boulders which had worn free and fallen from its looming surface during the passage of countless centuries. And sure enough the face of the mountain that went up beyond the keep did overhang in one place, and where the shadows should have been blackest below this overhang, instead there shone the faintest gleam of yellow light.

Flitting now from shadowed area to shadowed area like a pair of ghouls, the dreamers were brought up short by a sudden call. It was high-pitched, ululant – plainly the cry of a master to his minions, his hounds . . . or his snow-leopards.

'Hritta!' the warbling cry repeated. 'Nythlar!' And its echoes rebounded mockingly from distant peaks. Then, plainly audible (for their distance from the cave in the towering wall of rock was no more than a hundred yards), there came to the ears of the adventurers an angry grumbling and cursing; and finally the light retreated, leaving the entrance in darkness.

Still as statues Hero and Eldin stood, until the latter gave a quiet burp. 'I wonder,' he whispered, 'which one that was: Hritta or Nythlar? Something else: that didn't sound like the voice of any doddery old priest to me.'

'*Shh*!' Hero admonished, and they moved forward again.

Warily they entered the cave's mouth below the overhanging mountain peak and gradually their eyes adapted to the darkness. The cave wound away into the mountain, seemingly a natural tunnel whose ceiling was three times the height of a man and whose width was that of five men laid head to heel. Around the first bend a glimmering light showed, and soon the pair crept into a large chamber lighted by dimly flickering and smoky flambeaux. The place was bare, but iron staples supporting light chains were fixed in the walls. The chains were of ample length to meet across the width of the cave.

'That's where the snow-leopards spend their nights,' murmured Hero. 'Or rather, where they used to. Watchdogs, no less!'

'Umm!' answered Eldin. 'Strikes me we've already gone a long way toward disarming the old lad. What say you?'

'I say my hair is prickling,' the first answered. 'It's prickling all the way down my neck . . .'

For all Hero's premonition they went swiftly on, emerging in a few moments more into a second chamber. Here the rocky walls were hung with skins and the floor was covered in furs. A rough wooden table bore a flat platter of meat and a stone bottle. A second plate, with an empty goblet standing close at hand, bore the remains of a meal. Eldin cautiously approached the table, lifted the bottle and sniffed at its unstoppered neck. He smiled then, a thirsty smile, and licked his lips.

'Nectar!' he declared in a low rumble like a cat's purr, tilting the bottle and drinking deeply. Then his eyes went wide and he sighed his appreciation. 'By all that's beautiful, David, taste this!'

Curved blade at the ready, still staring warily all about at the shadows cast by sputtering flambeaux, the younger man crossed to the table and took the proffered bottle, automatically swigging at the sweet, strong liquid before whispering: 'Well, obviously he's had his supper, and doubtless he's now preparing for bed – or already tucked up. Strikes me he's not as wise as he might be by any means. Either that or we're not as clever as we think we are! Now then – where's that damned temple, eh?'

'Right!' Eldin agreed, taking back the bottle. 'We really can't afford to dally like this . . .'

When the bottle was empty to a drop and only the heady scent of the wine remained, then, spirits greatly bolstered, they left the second chamber behind them and continued deeper into the bowels of the mountain.

Occasionally as they went small tunnels would branch off to right and left, all terminating after only a few paces, so that following brief explorations they were obliged to continue down the main shaft. Several of these secondary tunnels were in use, being storage rooms for furs and skins, casks of oil, barrels of fruit and vegetables and other household items. The priest of the as yet unsighted 'temple,' whoever he was, seemed to live very well indeed according to the usual standards of the wandering dreamers.

Along the way, at intervals, the tunnel was illuminated by sputtering torches; but after a while these were more widely spaced out, so that there were periods of near-darkness. As they crept through one of these dark sections Eldin whispered:

'At this rate we'll soon come out through the other

side of the mountain!' to which Hero replied:

'It only seems a long way. But in any case, I don't think we have much farther to go.'

Now they moved a little slower, each touching a wall with outstretched hand while inner arm was linked with that of his companion. The tunnel here had narrowed down somewhat, but shortly they had to extend their inside arms as the cave widened out again. At the last only their fingertips touched; their swords were now sheathed and they carried their knives between clenched teeth; before each step the floor in front was explored by timidly probing, booted feet.

Then, suddenly, the walls widened farther yet and they paused amidst an almost unendurable darkness, conscious now of an inner tingling, of an all-enveloping sensation of extreme danger, and of – a presence!

A presence, aye; and even at the realization – as at a signal – the cave was at once dazzlingly illuminated! Brilliant, blinding bars of brightness criss-crossed the near-solid gloom about them in a coruscating blaze, and this in turn was replaced in the next instant by the steady yellow burning of a dozen wall-bracketed torches that burst almost simultaneously into flame.

Shielding their eyes against the sudden glare (and wondering at the same time how those twelve torches had been struck, since they stood in the presence of only one, small, wrinkled old man), the dreamers drew swords and held them threateningly out in front. Then, back to back, they turned in a slow circle, taking in every detail of the cave in which they now stood, alert for any strange, sudden or menacing movement in the hanging tapestries of the place.

IV

THINISTOR UDD AND ONE OTHER

The apartment, or 'temple,' was huge: fifty feet across and almost as high, with daggerlike stalactites hanging from the ceiling and squat stalagmites rising up through the luxuriant furs that lay three deep upon the floor. The walls were covered with black furs stitched together into drapes, and at intervals these were parted to frame the mouths of inner tunnels that led back into darkness. Two of these entrances were fitted with stout metal gates whose bars were inches thick.

Having satisfied themselves that no immediate danger threatened, none of any mundane nature at least, the pair faced the old man in his wizard's robes of red and black. He sat upon the cushioned stump of a stalagmite, tasselled conical hat upon his shrunken head, slender, knobbed black wand in his monkey's hand, peering at them sullenly through eyes which were yellow slits in his crinkled-parchment face.

Behind this evil-looking ancient, standing half in the shadow of a massive stalagmite, the carven figure of Yibb-Tstll loomed, overlooking all else in the temple. And over all else it was this monstrous effigy, despite being partly obscured, which primarily drew the wide eyes of the dreamers.

59

Of more or less manlike proportion, the – *thing* – had a head, a polished black lump atop its sloping shoulders of stone. Two eyes were frozen in oddly unnatural positions on the surface of the head: one was up near the top, the other was low, where the corner of a mouth might have been in a more nearly normal statue. The lower eye was green and shone with an inner luminosity – a massive emerald – but the other was of a reddish, bloody hue, and of the two it looked decidedly more real.

The narrowly sloping shoulders were cloaked, as was the bulky body beneath; but the cloak, carved of the same stalagmite stone as the god, was open in front to reveal many polished black breasts. This was an anomaly in itself since patently the figure was male. Beneath the cloak where it billowed in petrified rigidity, a cluster of stone night-gaunts, their wings folded, clung tightly, almost lovingly, to the unseen body of the god. The idol was a nightmare, made even more nightmarish by its height – which was almost three times that of a tall man!

Staring at the loathsome thing, the dreamers felt that they had left the sane world of dreams and now inhabited an alien dimension at the very rim of sanity. Their eyes went from the idol to the yellow eyes of the wizard, back to the idol, and finally –

'So!' the wizard-priest's thin, reedy voice – which yet hinted of an awful strength, a sorcerous power – drew their thoughts back to earth. 'And you two are the murderers of my pets, are you? The cruel butchers of poor Hritta and Nythlar? Well, welcome, dreamers – welcome to the Temple of Yibb-Tstll. I, Thinistor Udd, need not ask why you have come. For surely, like all the others recently ventured this way, you were sent by the Ossaran, Ebraim Borak, on behalf of my cousin Nyrass of Theelys, to steal my wand. And did you, too, like the others, think that it would be so very easy?'

'Old man, Thinistor Udd,' answered Hero, 'we've no quarrel with you. We're after the wand, that's true enough, but no need for any violence. And no magic, please, for our knives are surely faster than any of your spells!'

The two had separated as Hero talked, widening the distance between themselves, moving forward now with swords once more sheathed and replaced by long, curving knives.

Suddenly and for no apparent reason, Eldin blundered into a naked stump of stone and fell over it, his knife flying from his hand. At the same time Hero felt a dull ache spreading behind his eyes, clouding his mind. He, too, reeled and only managed to steady himself by leaning against a rocky knob that jutted up waist-high from the floor.

Eldin gropingly retrieved his knife and hauled himself to his feet. 'You were warned, wizard,' he rumbled. 'No magic!' His arm went back, curved blade gripped between thumb and forefinger, and –

'No!' cried Hero. 'No, Eldin – don't kill him!'

'Magic?' cackled the evil ancient. 'No, no, my friends from the waking world, not magic. Merely . . . a drug!'

'The wine!' gasped Eldin and Hero in unison.

'Aye, the wine. You see, I was expecting you. It's been a while since Borak sent me two such as you; indeed, you are long overdue. Ah, but this time he excels himself!'

'Borak!' snarled Eldin. And then – despite or perhaps because of one last attempt to throw his knife – the older dreamer gave a strangled cough, crumpled and sagged to his knees, fell face down among the furs. Hero took two more paces forward while the great cave seemed to revolve around him, then he too toppled, feeling nothing of the impact as his body brought a cloud of dust up from the fur-strewn floor . . .

Eldin was dying. He knew it from the very moment he awoke to the none-too-gentle slapping of tiny hands about his bearded face. There was a searing fire in his lungs, burning as never before, and all his great strength seemed to have evaporated within him, steamed out of his body by the consuming fire. He awoke with a great bloody cough bursting upward – which expired unuttered when scented, delicate fingers clamped firmly over his agonized mouth.

'Shh! Quiet, dreamer!' a girl's tremulous, fear-filled voice whispered. 'Hush, now – lest you wake Thinistor Udd!'

At that Eldin remembered where he was and all that had gone before. He opened his eyes and stared straight into those of an apparition. By the flickering flame of a small stone lamp he studied the girl. Slim as a willow twig, she was; blue-eyed and fair-skinned, with delicate features much like the aristocrats of Ilek-Vad; long-limbed for all that she was tiny, with soft golden hair falling about her bosom. In all – and dressed as she was in the flimsiest of gauzes and wraps, and certainly in any place other than this – she was a sight for sore eyes!

Eldin forced back the tearing coughs he felt welling inside to wheezingly ask: 'Who are you, girl? And what by all the gods are you doing here? Aye,' – he stared about at the small, featureless cave – 'and for that matter, where exactly is "here," eh?'

'You are in one of Thinistor's gated cells,' she told him. 'But hush, hush!'

She turned her attentions to David Hero who lay

nearby. Eldin tried to get up, discovered himself to be bound hand and foot, lay back again and watched the girl as she slapped Hero's drawn face until his eyes flickered open.

'Eh?' Hero said – then: 'What in the name of – ?'

'Shh!' the girl once more admonished. And again she suffered the burning gaze of a dreamer as Hero studied her where she sat upon her haunches. 'Do not struggle,' she said, as he began to strain against his ropes, 'for you'll only tighten Thinistor's bonds.'

'But what –' Hero began again, only to be cut off by:

'You are the wizard's captives and he would kill you – most horribly! Only I can save you, and only you can save me. If I have your promise that you'll take me with you, then I'll help you to escape.'

'Done!' said Eldin at once. 'But only set us free.'

'Aye,' agreed Hero, 'you have our word. But come, loosen these bonds. And while you're about it you can tell us what you know of Thinistor Udd.'

The knots were tight and the ropes thin and strong, but nevertheless, the girl worked hard and fast with small deft fingers. She worked on Hero first, and as her fingers flew so she talked:

'My name is Aminza Anz, and I was taken by a gaunt from the balcony of my father's home in Ilek-Vad. That was almost a year ago, since when I've been here. At first I thought that the gaunt would eat me, but I don't know if they do eat.'

Hero nodded. 'We know,' he said. 'Gaunts have no faces, and so no mouths. Neither has Yibb-Tstll a mouth, if we can judge by that idol we saw in Thinistor's temple.'

'True, and Yibb-Tstll is the Lord of Gaunts.'

'Interesting,' Hero mused.

'For goodness sake go *on*, girl!' grunted Eldin, impatient of interruptions.

'Anyway,' Aminza quickly continued, 'I wasn't eaten but brought here. It took the gaunt all of three nights to get me here, resting in mountain caves by day and only journeying under the stars. Sometimes he'd fly me half-way up to the moon, and then for hours we'd glide and glide where shoals of hideous, shapeless drifting *things* groped and pawed and tried to wrest me from the gaunt's awful grasp.'

'The larvae of the Other Gods!' said Hero, his voice hushed. 'I've heard mention of them before.'

'Perhaps,' Aminza answered, then grunted with delight as one of the knots came loose behind Hero's back. Without pause she started on another.

By now Eldin was fidgeting as though he had fleas. 'Go on, lass,' he urged. 'Can't you get on? These ropes are cutting me in pieces!'

'Well,' she went on, 'I was asleep when we got here, and when I woke up – there was Thinistor Udd.' She shuddered.

'And he's kept you here ever since, eh?' asked Hero. 'But why did he have you brought here in the first place? Has he been . . . bothering you?'

'Pardon?'

'Does he take you to bed, lass?' Eldin was more direct.

'No, no,' she shuddered again. 'But he looks at me a lot and makes me dance. And sometimes he . . . touches me.'

'Huh!' the gnarled dreamer grunted. 'He's past it, then.'

'Only his body is old,' she answered as yet another knot came loose in her hands. 'His mind is sharp as a razor.'

'It's a razor I'll be taking to his scrawny throat as soon as you've got us loose,' Eldin replied. 'The razor edge of my knife – if I can find it!'

Hero sniffed disgustedly. 'You didn't really think he'd leave us our weapons, did you?'

'Don't go snapping at me, lad,' Eldin rumbled, 'or by –'

'*Shh!*' Hero fiercely hissed. 'Hell's teeth, Eldin – you'll have the roof down on us with your bellowing!' Then, to the girl, he said: 'And did he lock you up with us, Aminza? Surely he was taking a chance?'

'No,' she answered. 'Indeed, he forbade me to come near. But you are my one chance for freedom. Soon he would do with me as he does with the others. I was small enough to squeeze in through the bars – but you two will have to break down the gate.' She gave a little grunt of triumph, said 'There!' – and at last Hero's hands were free.

'Work on Eldin,' the young dreamer told her. 'I'll free my own feet . . . as soon as there's an ounce of blood flowing in these numb hands of mine!' He began to rub at his hands, working life back into them. 'Gods, girl, but I could kiss you – aye, and more than that – if things were a little different.'

Aminza said nothing but her blush could be seen even in the flickering lamplight. As she started work on the ropes that bound Eldin, the older man asked:

'What others were you talking about? And what was it Thinistor did to them?'

For a moment she paused in her task to peer at him, and again she shuddered. 'Other prisoners,' she finally answered. 'Other men that the gaunts bring him, or who come here from Theelys, sent by –'

'By a treacherous Ossaran dog!' Eldin cut in.

Aminza nodded. 'Thinistor, he . . . he sucks at them like a vampire with his wand. He changes them to little bags of bones, which he then feeds to his snow-leopards. You see, he's determined to regain his youth. That's why he came here in the first place, why he discovered a way into the Keep of the First Ones. He brought things out of there with him, secrets the First Ones knew.'

'Secrets?' Hero repeated, finally freeing his feet. 'What sort of secrets?'

'Things that drove him mad!' she answered.

'His wand?' Hero pressed.

'No. He found that hidden in these caves. From the keep he brought knowledge of strange magicks. He knows how to call up Yibb-Tstll – or so he says.'

The dreamers looked at each other, then back to the girl. 'How do you know all this, Aminza?' asked Hero.

'He told me so himself. Often he rambles on, especially when the moon is round and full in the night sky. For years he has worked to discover the secrets of the First Ones, and now he finally draws close to understanding them. His search for youth is only the first step. After that . . . the magick of the First Ones will make him the greatest sorcerer in all the dreamlands – and the cruellest!'

'What makes you think he's close, girl?' asked Eldin.

'I've seen him when he's drained someone,' she answered with a grimace. 'For a little while he's young again. Then – swiftly he grows old! With you two he plans to stay young forever. After that, strong and daring, he'll go back into the Keep of the First Ones. Who can say what he'll bring out next?'

'Who, indeed?' echoed Hero thoughtfully.

'Using us he'll stay young forever?' Eldin suspiciously repeated her words. 'You mean he plans to –?'

'Little bags of bones,' Hero grimly cut in. 'Aye, well, I'm not quite ready for that yet. Come on, toss

your feet over here, old friend. It's time we were loose
and on our way.' To Aminza he said: 'Where's
Thinistor now, girl? And where does he keep his
gaunts?'

'He sleeps. Such are his thaumaturgies that he
needs a great deal of sleep. When he wakes he will
draw strength from Yibb-Tstll's idol – which is an
avatar of the true demon-god – and then . . .' she
paused uncertainly.

'Then it's our turn, eh?' they asked as one.

For answer she nodded. 'So I believe. As for the
gaunts: why, you've seen them for yourselves!'

'Eh?' Hero frowned. 'You mean those stone horrors
hanging from the idol's teats?'

'Indeed. When they are needed, Thinistor . . .
wakes them!'

The dreamers stared at each other.

'David, I fear we're deep in nightmares now,' said
Eldin, 'and much as I know you're against murder,
this time it seems –'

'– We'll have to kill him,' Hero finished it for him.

The other gravely nodded. 'Right. There are too
damned many wizards in dreamland anyway. And the
sane ones are bad enough!'

V

THE TAKING OF
THE EYE

'Damn it, girl, you said he was asleep!' Eldin accused in a loud whisper. 'He's the liveliest sleepwalker I've ever seen!'

'He must have been eager to start,' Aminza answered in his ear, her voice a mere breath. 'Certainly he was asleep when I left my bed. Something may have woken him up.'

'Perhaps he sensed your game,' said Hero, 'and discovered your absence.'

'No, no,' she replied. 'For I made up my bed to appear as I were in it. Besides, he would have come for me and called me out.'

The three of them were crouched in the shadows at the gate of the tunnel that led back to their prison cavelet. In the main cave, through the bars of the gate and by the light of flambeaux, Thinistor Udd could be seen to be engaged in magic. His back was turned to them where he stood half-hidden by a stalagmite before Yibb-Tstll's idol. His arms were stretched high and wide over his head and in one hand he held his knobbed wand.

His voice crackled like subdued lightning in the confines of the cave, and as he chanted his alien discords so, occasionally, he would strike the stony gaunts where they clung beneath the folds of Yibb-Tstll's cloak. Whenever he did this bursts of brilliant white fire would go slanting off, dying before they could strike either ceiling or walls.

'What's he doing?' asked Eldin.

'He draws strength from the idol,' Aminza answered. 'See how he swells up when his wand strikes fire? Also, he is waking the gaunts. He always wakes them before – before . . .' She stared at the dreamers, eyes wide in a death-white face.

'Before he drains someone?' asked Hero.

She nodded. 'The gaunts go out to guard the plateau and the mouth of the cave, making sure there are no intruders and that Thinistor will not be disturbed.'

Even as she spoke a fantastic thing began to happen. The god's stone cloak grew blurred in appearance, as if viewed through smoke, and its central parting seemed for all the world to widen, wholly revealing the gaunts where they now writhed fitfully as they clung to the god's monstrous body. Then, one by one – stone things no longer but rubbery creatures from the mind of a madman – they fell from the idol like strangely ripened fruit, opening their wings and speeding in a flock round and about the cave's walls and ceiling. A moment more of this wild circling until, as at a signal, they made for the exit tunnel and disappeared into it in a great flapping of leathery wings.

'We must act now!' Aminza hissed. 'A moment more and he will be too strong for you. Look – ah! – *too late*!'

For Thinistor had turned from the idol's uncertainly wavering figure, had seen the three where they crouched at the barred gate, and his yellow eyes were tinged red with fires of hell. He pointed his wand . . .

'*Now*!' cried Eldin and Hero together, stepping

70

back a pace before slamming their massive frames against the metal bars of the gate. The bars bent from their combined weight – chains snapped and hinges sheared – and the gate went down in a cloud of dust and stony debris. The dreamers fell with the gate as Thinistor's bolt passed harmlessly over their heads. It missed Aminza by the breadth of a hot kiss and exploded in white fury in the depths of the prison.

'If a bolt strikes you,' the girl screamed, 'it will not kill you outright but suck you dry, carrying your strength back to Thinistor!'

Hearing her, Hero rolled to one side as a second bolt seared the air scant inches away, spending itself in a blazing ball of white sparks against the draped wall of the cave. Eldin was springing forward, last dregs of strength powering him, carrying a long metal stave snatched up from the debris of the gate. Aminza, too, played her part, sprinting for the shelter of a knobby stalagmite, distracting the enraged wizard.

And indeed Thinistor, no longer shrunken but swelled out with sorcerous power, was enraged – and confused. His passion saved the three, for in its throes his bolts flew wide and scored no hits. Then, too late, the wizard saw the iron stave where it flew at him from the hand of the older dreamer. He saw it, shrank back, hurled one last, useless bolt, and screamed one shrill scream as the spiked head of the stave impaled him and threw him down. He fell, clutching the iron where it entered the center of his body, and his wand of power went bouncing harmlessly across the covered floor. By the time the three had converged warily upon the wizard's once more shrunken form, his eyes had closed and he lay still.

'There's no blood,' observed Eldin, panting from his exertions and clutching painfully at his chest.

'Wizards don't bleed,' said Hero.

'You must be quick now,' Aminza grasped their

71

arms. 'Soon the gaunts will return, which they must before the idol can once more turn to true stone.'

'But surely the idol *is* stone?' Hero frowned.

'No, it's half and half. See –' and she pointed. Sure enough, the outline of the hideous effigy still wavered, and it seemed to the dreamers that its red eye gazed evilly down upon them. The emerald eye, on the other hand, still beckoned enticingly; and now there was nothing to stop them from taking it.

'Our weapons!' cried Eldin, spotting their knives and swords where they lay wrapped in a skin on the floor.

'Good!' said Hero, his voice much harder than its norm. 'Give me my knife. Mountains and snow-leopards – gaunts and mad wizards – demon gods and what all: *damn them to the nineteen hells!* We came for the wand and now we have it. Aye, and that great jewel's coming with us, too, when we leave!' He pointed at Yibb-Tstll's emerald eye.

'Well spoken, lad,' wheezed Eldin, sitting down heavily on Thinistor's stony throne. 'But that's a climb you'll need to make on your own. This old fellow's winded. Girl,' he grasped Aminza's wrist. 'Is there nothing for a man to drink in this place?'

While Aminza found an unbroken bottle of wine for Eldin, Hero climbed the carved folds of Yibb-Tstll's cloak. He was aware of the unpleasant, vibrating *feel* of the warm and slimy stone under his hands, aware, too, of the half life with which this monstrous lump of rock seemed imbued – which made its surface appear fuzzy to his eyes and full of trapped motion, like a frozen whirlpool – but at last he perched with one foot in a high fold of cloak and one arm thrown about the horror's neck. Then he took his knife in his free hand and started to prise the jewel loose. He dug around the edges of the socket, where the stone seemed strangely soft, until finally he could stab the knife in deep and lever the great emerald free.

As he did so, suddenly it seemed to him that the idol convulsed in a kind of spasm – of agony, perhaps? – and at that he gave an involuntary shudder and jumped free to land catlike on the furs at the foot of the carven effigy. The jewel had fallen, too, directly into Aminza's hands where she stood waiting. Grimacing, Hero wiped his hands on his brown jacket and took back the huge jewel. He took out a coarse handkerchief, formed it into a little sack around the emerald and tied it to his belt.

By then, despite the fact that Eldin was a half bottle of red wine heavier, the older dreamer was back on his feet and raring to go. To the girl he said: 'Aminza, does Thinistor have any other goodies of value lying around? A treasure chest or two, perhaps?'

'He has a lot of money somewhere,' she answered, 'but I've been here for a year and never found it yet. Perhaps he's hidden it in the great keep. And of course, there's his wand of power . . .'

'I'll take that,' said Eldin, catching up the wand from where it lay at his feet. But no sooner was the wand in his hand than a great blue spark leaped from its knob to strike him in the forehead, standing his hair on end and hurling him backward head over heels in a somersault from Thinistor's stalagmite throne. He let out a yell of shock and anguish as he fell in a tangle to the furs of the floor.

Then, as Eldin dizzily propped himself up on his elbows and shook his head to clear it, Hero stepped over and gingerly tried his luck with the fallen wand. Before his fingers could even touch it, however, small bright sparks flew up in warning, causing him to snatch back his hand. 'Damn thing just doesn't want to be taken!' he snarled.

'Then we'll have to leave it,' Eldin grunted. 'And in any case, wands are for wizards. If Borak still wants it, he'll just have to come after it himself – if he's still capable when I've finished with him!'

'Aye, too true,' Hero readily agreed. He was fully recovered now from his funny turn with the idol, but still he kept a wary eye on the mutilated face of the stone god where it stood half in shadow. 'Anyway, we have this monster's eye, and I say that's treasure enough. So let's be on our way.' To Aminza he said: 'Can you climb, girl?'

'I can try,' she answered.

'Good. The Great Bleak Mountains are high and it's a long way down if you fall!'

And so they quickly set off along the main tunnel that led back to the lofty plateau and its sentinel Keep of the First Ones.

This time they moved faster through the tunnel, lighting the way with torches taken from the flambeaux in the temple, and in a very short time they emerged from under the overhanging peak onto the plateau. Dawn was coming up over the edge of dreamland and with it a chill and moaning wind that blew the torches out, leaving the trio shrouded in a cold and deceptive half-light. The dreamers headed straight for the keep, intending to skirt its great base and return down the mountain along the same route they had used to climb it. Aminza, now warmly wrapped, stepped nimbly between them, almost aglow with the gladness of being free at last from her ordeal. Then, as they entered the shade of the looming keep –

– *Bat-wings beating, and a cloud of leathery gaunts settling all around them!* The things had been waiting in shadows high on the face of the keep, and now they buffeted with their wings, punched, kicked and gouged with their rubbery paws.

Swords whispering and slicing, knives stabbing, the dreamers fought back to the best of their ability – ah, but they were not used to looking after a woman! Aminza, having no weapons of her own with which to fight, was snatched aloft by a pair of gaunts and whirled away, back toward the overhang and the cave it shadowed. Her cries came back to the two as they battled desperately, fighting for their very lives.

And abruptly as the fight had begun it was over. The gaunts lifted up and flapped away, leaving three of their number behind, stretched lifeless on the cold, snow-patched ground. Against a brightening sky Hero stood tall and roared his frustration.

'Damn and blast all creation!' he cried, waving his sword. 'Now we'll have to go back for her. Eldin . . . what –?' He quickly kneeled and held out his hand to the older man. 'What's wrong, old friend? Did you get a clout?'

'My bloody pumps!' the other wheezed, spitting redly on a patch of snow. 'They're coming apart, I'm sure. You go back, and all speed. I'll get my wind and follow. I'll wait for you at the mouth of the cave. Sorry, David – and good luck!'

But Hero was already gone, racing for the overhang, white teeth gritted and sword at the ready, the weight of Yibb-Tstll's emerald eye jouncing against his thigh . . .

Aminza, buffeted almost unconscious by the wings of the two gaunts as they sped with her back along the tunnel toward the temple of Yibb-Tstll, did not see what passed her moving in the opposite direction. This was as well, for while the god's stone idol was a sight evil enough by any standard, Yibb-Tstll in the flesh was a thousand times worse! She knew, however, as soon as she regained her senses where her captors had tossed her to the floor of the temple, what had happened.

Thinistor Udd, though gravely injured, had not been dead when they had left him in the temple. Recovering, he had used his wand to gain strength from the morbid idol. This was all too plain from the way he now sat with his back propped against the base of his throne, wand to hand, darkly stained stave beside him where he had lain it after dragging it from his body. The idol's absence spoke for itself, that and the trail of dishevelled furs that led across the floor of the cave and into the exit tunnel.

Now, as Aminza lifted herself onto one elbow, Thinistor looked at her. Glistening droplets of sweat formed on his bald, yellowed pate and forehead to roll down and wet his sickly, agonized face; but his yellow eyes were bright and evil as ever. From the wand he held in his clawlike hand a greenish light streamed out, following the trail of disturbed furs and disappearing into the main tunnel. Aminza knew that Thinistor guided the god through this thread of alien energy, knew also that he had sent that hideous Being out to bring back her friends from the waking world. To bring them back – or to kill them!

'Did you think to escape from Thinistor Udd so easily, girl?' he whispered through cracked lips which scarcely moved, so great was his pain. 'I can see that you did. Well, old Thinistor's not dead yet, not by a thousand years or more! And you'll pay for your treachery, you may count on it. As for your friends: they've seen their last morning in dreamland, I fear. They took Yibb-Tstll's eye, which displeased him greatly. Even if I wanted to I couldn't save them now – and I don't want to!'

'*No!*' he cautioned, as Aminza made to rise. 'Don't

76

move, girl, or they'll have you quick as a flash!' He cast his eyes up to the ceiling where clung the two gaunts which had recaptured her.

As she sank down again to the floor of the temple, Thinistor laughed. 'Aye, best to do as you're told. Gaunts have no faces but they're manlike enough in other ways, eh, girl?' And despite his obvious agony he cackled mercilessly before returning his gaze to the weave of green light where it flowed from his wand . . .

VI
THE DARK GOD WALKS!

Reaching the cave entrance under the overhang, Hero paused. The bristling of the short hairs at the base of his neck warned him that apart from all else there was something here completely outside human experience, dreaming or otherwise, something which never should be in any sane or ordered universe. A wind was rushing from the tunnel, carrying with it a rotten smell that had him pinching his nostrils in disgust. He stood, as at the lip of a tomb freshly opened after many centuries, and his eyes widened as he saw, deep in the gloom of the cave, a greenish light swelling and brightening even as he watched. Something was coming down the tunnel from Yibb-Tstll's temple, and the way the dreamer's feet suddenly seemed rooted to the earth, he knew that whatever it was it boded ill for any merely human adversary.

Dawn's light was brightening rapidly now, and the wind from the west had slackened slightly. Incapable of motion and feeling that chill but gentle wind on his back, Hero's eyes bugged as he watched the green glow pulsing closer still and his inner mind screamed for him to take some defensive action, to run and put distance between himself and the unknown horror. Then, breaking his paralysis –

'David!' came Eldin's cry, carried on the wind that blew from the looming keep. 'Man, come back and give me a hand. I can't handle all of them myself!' At that the younger dreamer half-turned, saw his companion less than a hundred yards away, hard pressed by the flight of gaunts which had returned and now hovered about him where he slashed and hacked. Alone, he could barely hold them at bay; and slowly but surely they were driving him back toward the cave's entrance, back to whatever it was that came in greenish rottenness, looming ever larger from the depths of the tunnel.

Hero cast one more glance into the gloomy bowels of the mountain, enough to make out the outline of the *thing* that moved there in its nimbus of emerald fire, and then his feet seemed to grow wings as he sped back to Eldin and joined him in fighting off the gaunts.

'What now, lad?' Eldin panted, his face white in the half-light and drawn with awful exertions. 'Back to the cave?'

'No,' gasped Hero, skewering a gaunt and withdrawing his blade before the dead creature could crash to earth at his feet. 'I've seen what's coming after us. I think it's Yibb-Tstll himself. And these damned gaunts are simply here to slow us down!'

Eldin roared his anger as one of the rubbery monsters fell onto his back, almost throwing him from his feet. He leaned forward and Hero lopped off the horror's blind head. On the next instant, as the carcass of the headless creature slid from the older man's straining frame, the remaining gaunts lifted skyward in a concerted throbbing of wings. For a second the two dreamers stared at each other wide-eyed, then gazed back toward the cave beneath the overhang.

Yibb-Tstll's bulk was emerging into the still dim

light, surrounded by a greenish glow, and one look at
that black god of horror was almost too much for the
adventurers to bear. Eldin grasped Hero's arm and
croaked: 'The cliffs, quick! We must go the way we
came!'

'No,' the other answered, gulping air into lungs
which felt starved, galvanizing a body that seemed
utterly unmanned. 'No, the gaunts would pick us off
the cliff like flies off a wall . . .'

'What, then?'

'The final crest. Perhaps we'll have room to fight
the gaunts off up there, and we might just be able to
start an avalanche and –'

'– And send that great horror to hell! Yes, lad, I
like your idea. But the way I feel, you might yet end up
seeing this thing through on your own!' And Eldin
coughed up a great red blotch and spat it onto a patch
of snow.

Inadvertently, as they fled for the slope that
climbed to the final crest of snow, the two found
themselves drawn to look back again at the thing that
pursued them: Yibb-Tstll – a loathsomeness from the
dead spaces between the stars – whose living visage
made his previously stony aspect seem almost warm
and friendly by comparison!

Greenly illumined, Yibb-Tstll seemed to flow tower-
ingly, purposefully toward them. The god's feet, or
whatever other members propelled him, were hidden
beneath his billowing cloak. His eye – that *single* eye,
where recently there had been two – was now alive,
redly glistening, quick with a hideous mobility. It slid
over the surface of the demon-god's pulpy face with a
swift and apparently aimless motion.

The empty socket which once had housed the other
eye – the great emerald that now jounced against
Hero's thigh – moved in similarly pointless circles

and dripped a black pus that steamed where it splashed on the stony ground. But if the movements of Yibb-Tstll's hideous orb and its companion socket seemed aimless, the determined way in which he now moved after the dreamers most certainly was not!

What few gaunts remained had gathered themselves to the huge monster and disappeared beneath his weirdly fluttering cloak. Their presence there did not, however, slow him down, and for all his vast bulk he flowed effortlessly up the final slope, obliterating the tracks that the dreamers had left in the thawing snow.

Now, approaching the crest of the snow-ridge, the two struggled through clinging, knee-deep snow that drenched their legs, slowing and tiring them until at last, almost exhausted, they reached the very top. And there they were finally obliged to call a halt; for at their feet, as if some giant had sliced both snow and mountain with a massive sword, a sheer fall of rock went down and down for thousands of feet into mighty, misty deeps.

Before them the seemingly bottomless chasm – where the morning mists now boiled upward, climbing the sheer face of rock toward them – and to the rear the lumbering god of unknown dimensions beyond dreamland, bent upon the recovery of his emerald eye . . . and certainly upon less mentionable things.

'Thinistor Udd lives!' croaked Eldin. 'See, the green light follows the god like a long trail, winding away back to his temple. It was the wizard sent Yibb-Tstll after us.'

'Whoever sent him, I'll jump before I give myself up to *that*!' Hero pantingly declared. As he spoke a warm glow bathed their backs: the sun, risen at last on what could well be their last morning in Earth's dreamland.

And still the horror came on, his stench reaching them like the breath of an open tomb as he climbed the slope of snow. Down on all fours went the adventurers, frantically shaping great balls of wet snow which they propelled down the slope toward Yibb-Tstll's hideous form. Gathering snow and momentum as they rolled, the balls smashed into the monster god with the impact of boulders; but what they had in weight they lacked in consistency, flying apart and tumbling past the lumbering giant in wetly bouncing fragments that avalanched down to the plateau of the keep. And Yibb-Tstll was impeded not at all.

Less than fifty feet separated the pair at bay from that awful Being when the latter's cloak suddenly burst open to release upon the beleaguered dreamers the few remaining gaunts. Balanced precariously on a narrow and infirm ribbon of snow, Hero and Eldin were hardly in a good position to do battle with the creatures; it was as much as they could do to protect themselves. And still the terrible form of Yibb-Tstll came on, his single eye sliding over his face more rapidly now, perhaps in nameless anticipation . . .

Aminza knew she dared wait no longer. The look on Thinistor's face told her that much. Seated with his back against the base of his stalagmite throne, the wizard's yellow eyes were wide and full of mad delight, and the corners of his mouth curved upward in an awful smile. Aminza had little doubt that in some magical way he 'saw' whatever sight presented itself to Yibb-Tstll, carried back to him, perhaps, by the greenly weaving umbilicus of light that still streamed from Thinistor's wand. If that was the case then her dreamer friends must be in a fearsome plight.

And if they were done for, then so was Aminza. She feared the wizard, yes, and also the pair of gaunts that silently clung to the cave's ceiling; but the wild men of the waking world that she had befriended were her last hope, her one chance for freedom.

Lithe as a cat, in one flowing movement she came to her feet and flew at Thinistor, snatching up the heavy stave from where it lay beside him and whirling it once about her head. She heard the throb of rubbery wings as the shadows of the gaunts fell across her; but then, before the wizard could do more than turn his feral eyes on her, she swung the metal stave against his head.

Thinistor gave a single shriek – high and bubbling – as the ancient bones of his skull caved in where the stave embedded itself in soft brain . . . and then all was chaos!

The greenly glowing light dimmed and flickered; one gaunt, instantly frozen in stone, crashed down to the floor with a shock that shivered it to fragments; the other smashed blindly into the cave's wall, its wings snapping like chalk as it too returned to its stony state. Then the green light flickered one last time and, with a crackling of alien energies, snapped out. Thinistor dropped his wand and fell to one side. He lay still, his yellow eyes wide and blind, accusingly staring at Aminza as his brains trickled out of his shattered skull.

VII
THE LIVING EYE

In the same moment that Aminza rose up to hurl herself at Thinistor, up on the snow-ridge Yibb-Tstll had come within reach of the dreamers. Now, as Eldin skewered the last of the gaunts through its neck, sending its lifeless body spinning into the awesome chasm, the demon-god reached out from beneath his billowing cloak three green and black things which might have been arms, each terminating in seven slimy worms which were perhaps fingers.

Hero immediately slashed at one of these loathsome appendages with his curved blade of Kled, but his weapon simply bounced off. The monster's flesh was completely impervious to weapons of Earth's dreamland. The seven long 'fingers' of that uninjured 'hand' wrapped around Hero's head, forcing him to his knees, while the other two arms reached for Eldin.

Utterly exhausted, the older dreamer miraculously avoided Yibb-Tstll's slimy grasp and went down on his knees beside his companion. As he did so his fingers touched the kerchief-wrapped gem where it hung from Hero's belt. He tore at the bundle, crying:

'It's your eye, isn't it? You've come for your damned eye!' And as Hero fought to tear loose the vile fingers which groped to get into his eyes, his mouth, nostrils and ears, so Eldin ripped open the snow-wet bundle and clutched its contents to his heaving chest – for a moment only!

For the gem was a gem no longer, nor was it green and hard. It was wet and soft as jelly, and it was red! It was an eye – a *living* eye – the twin of the loathsome orb that vacillated even now over Yibb-Tstll's hideous face!

Instinctively, or as if inspired, Eldin squeezed the thing in his massive hands, and instantly the demon-god snatched back his three writhing pseudopods. For a moment Yibb-Tstll seemed to throb and expand – in rage, perhaps, or pain – but then his cloak flew wide and allowed the stunned dreamers to peer within . . . at a writhing mass of sucking mouths, lashing pseudopods and heaving black breasts! Right up to the two flowed the horror from the stars, and in another moment his cloak had started to close about them. Then –

'Take your damned eye!' yelled Eldin, and with his last ounce of strength he hurled the softly plastic thing into the horror's face. With a sickening squelching sound the eye flew into and filled the empty socket. In that same instant the demon-god shuddered to a halt. All motion went out of the huge figure; the cloak's eery undulations ceased; the vastly lumbering being turned stony gray and its prodigal eye flashed green once more!

Whatever Yibb-Tstll's living weight, it in no way compared to his weight as a stone thing. The ridge shuddered as a jagged, zig-zagging crack appeared in the thick crust of snow directly beneath Eldin where he crouched. As the gap widened he lost his balance and tumbled into it, falling face down on solid rock. Then there came the roar of avalanching boulders and snow and Eldin saw the ridge swept clean as the petrified god began to somersault backward down the steep slope, flying into fragments as he went.

In less than a minute all was still except for the wracking coughs that shattered an almost unnatural silence. Eldin, when he had himself under control, turned his face from the scene of devastation down on the plateau of the keep, staring into the disk of the rising sun. 'David,' he croaked, scanning the empty ridge. Then he blinked his eyes against the dazzle of sunlight and stared harder, unable to comprehend that indeed the summit was naked, a ridge of scarred and empty rock.

'David!' Eldin roared, hearing his mighty shout of horror and despair echoing away and down into unknown inner vaults. For a moment there was utter silence, then –

'Never mind the shouting, old lad!' came his friend's hoarse cry from beyond the rim of the ridge. 'Just get on down to the caves and fetch a rope – and be quick about it!'

Eldin laughed wildly at that and crawled to the lip of the chasm. Fifty feet below, sprawled in the branches of a cleft-grown shrub green with spring's buds, David Hero looked up with white face and wide eyes. Below him the face of the cliff seemed to go down forever, was lost in cloud at an indeterminate depth.

'Hang on, lad,' Eldin cried. 'I'll be back, never fear. And David –'

'Yes?'

'Don't go away!'

In fact it was Aminza climbed the ridge to haul Hero to safety. She had met Eldin as he staggered on useless legs toward the cave, had helped him into the warm tunnel, covered him with furs, poured wine down him until he could talk coherently. Then she had found a rope and gone to look for Hero.

Since then a month had gone by and with it the very last traces of snow from the heights. Since then, too, Hero and Aminza had searched diligently among the fragments of stalagmitic rock at the foot of the final rise, discovering nothing of Yibb-Tstll's emerald eye. Which was probably just as well.

Now the three of them stood together at the foot of the great keep, weighed down with necessaries, fit and rested and ready to move on – even Eldin, ruddy with health, whose painful coughing had not been heard for well over a week.

'I still don't understand it,' the older dreamer grumbled. 'There was I, fit to die – and here I am now, strong as a horse!'

'Thinistor's medicine,' Aminza answered with a laugh. 'If I've told you once, I've told you a dozen times. When the great gaunt first brought me here, I, too, was near to death. It was a result of all that flying in the cold night air. Thinistor gave me the same elixir I gave to you – with the same result. We were both made well! So you see, some good came out of that old devil Thinistor after all.'

'Indeed it did,' Eldin growled, giving the girl a hug that near cracked her ribs. He turned to the younger man, strangely silent as he stared up at the massive wall of the keep. 'What's on your mind, David?'

'Uh? Oh, I was just wondering . . .'

'About what? The keep?' Eldin frowned and took the other's arm. 'Now just a minute, lad –'

But Hero shook himself free and turned to his companions with blazing, excited eyes. 'Why not?' he demanded. 'Thinistor found a way in, didn't he? Why shouldn't we? Who's to say what we'd find in there?'

Eldin looked at the girl and shrugged. 'You did say

that the wizard had a lot of money hidden away somewhere, Aminza. Well, perhaps he kept it in the keep.'

'So,' she answered fatalistically. 'Where do we go
from here?'

Her companions looked at each other and grinned.

'We have a way of making decisions at times like
this,' said Hero, taking out a golden tond. He handed
the coin to Eldin. 'Are you with us, girl?'

'Do I have a choice?'

'We'll do as you wish, Aminza,' Eldin immediately
answered. 'We owe you that much at least.'

'Yes, but you'd never forgive me,' she returned.
'So – let's do it! Let it all rest on the toss of a coin.'

For a long moment the three stared into each others'
eyes. 'We do have a little unfinished business with a
certain Ossaran,' Hero murmured.

'Aye,' Eldin agreed, 'but it's not as if we'll be here
forever. Two or three days at most . . .' They looked
up at the looming keep, and as the sun passed behind
it so its shadow began to fall upon them.

'Heads we stay,' said Hero, breaking the silence.

'And tails –' Eldin began.

'– Means Theelys,' Aminza finished, 'and a ship
bound for Ilek-Vad for me.'

Hero took a deep breath and flipped the coin high,
and the triangular tond glinted as it flashed out of
shadow and into sunlight, before falling to the earth
at their feet . . .

PART THREE

I
IN THE KEEP

'Hey!' yelled Hero as he raced in through the entrance of the overhung cave. 'Hey, Eldin, Aminza! I've found it, the way into the keep! I've –' He skidded to a halt, eyes going wide as he took in the scene. There they sat on a pile of soft furs, Eldin the Wanderer swilling wine from a stone bottle, one arm carelessly over Aminza's shoulder, the hand fondling a breast through thin silk; and the girl snuggling up to the great oaf, nuzzling his leathery cheek, counting the forest of hairs on his massive chest.

Startled, they looked up at him for a moment, then Eldin got to his feet. 'Ah, David. It's as well you've discovered our little secret, er, for we'd have to tell you sooner or later. But Aminza and I, we're going to be wed. You'll be best man, of course . . . Won't you?'

'Eh?' Hero shook himself, blew dust off his brown jacket. 'Oh, certainly, but –'

'You look puzzled, lad,' the older man rumbled, placing what he meant to be a fatherly hand on Hero's shoulder. Hero, who stood somewhat taller than Eldin and wasn't all *that* much younger, hated it when his friend took on that tone of voice, pretending a paternal interest. 'Is it so strange that the little baggage should want to bed me down?'

'You asked me,' Aminza sweetly interrupted. 'Remember?'

Hero pointed vaguely behind him out of the mouth of the cave at the great Keep of the First Ones where it loomed massively across the high plateau. 'Look, it doesn't matter who asked who, whom or which – I just –'

'Of course we'll have to fight for her,' the scarfaced Eldin scowled. 'It's the custom in certain villages where I've lodged.'

What? Hero howled, hopping impatiently now from one foot to the other. 'Look, it's you who wants her, not I. If your engagement calls for blood-letting, you'll just have to bang your thick head on the wall of the cave once or twice. That should do the trick. Meanwhile –'

'You disappoint me, David,' Eldin cut him off. 'Haven't you learned any of dreamland's customs? The best man to be always –'

'To hell with the best man to be!' Hero roared. 'You sex-besotted clown – I'll –' And he swung a rock-hard fist at the other's head.

'That's better,' Eldin grunted, grinning as he side-stepped the angry blow to deliver a lightning ham with a satisfying *thok* on Hero's jaw. The younger dreamer was lifted an inch off his feet and thrown across the cave mouth, banging his head on a stone where he landed on his back.

Hero shot to his feet, eyes turning bloodshot now, curved Kledan blade growing almost magically from his hand. The other backed off a step, made placating motions with his hands, said: 'Easy, lad, easy. Enough is enough. That's all the ceremony calls for: the challenge and the answer. Nothing extravagant.' He turned from Hero and hugged Aminza to him. 'The first marrying priest we find –' he started – and stopped short. His great head snapped round and his black eyebrows peaked in the middle as he stared at his friend from the waking world. 'Did you say –?'

Hero cast his eyes to the ceiling of the cave and his sword with a clang to its dusty floor. 'What's the use?' he asked of no one in particular, disgustedly dabbing at a trickle of blood from where he'd bit a lip when Eldin struck him.

'You found the way in?' the big man whispered, then roared, 'Where? Where?' He unhanded Aminza and bounded across the cave, peering out and away at the hugely looming keep, yellow now with sharp sunlight.

'There,' said Hero, slitting his eyes and pointing at the distantly featureless face of stone. 'Between the stars.'

'I see no –' said Eldin, craning his bull neck.

Then, fists clenched into a club, Hero hit him on the back of his head. Down went Eldin like a felled oak, face down in the dust. 'Now do you see them?' Hero grinned. But the other merely groaned and spat out dirt.

'Boys will be buffoons,' said Aminza, moving lithely across the cave mouth to offer Eldin her hand. 'Did you really find the entrance, David?'

'I did,' he grinned again. 'While you two were eyeing and sighing back here, I rediscovered old Thinistor's secret. I found the way into the great keep. The old wizard had marked his route and I stumbled across it. We were wasting our time seeking a door in the base of the keep; the entrance is halfway up its face!'

'Then we'll need ropes,' Eldin grunted, squinting his eyes and tenderly fingering the back of his head. 'What did you find inside? Thinistor's gold? Treasure? Marvels and wonders?'

Hero shook his head. 'I found a maze,' he answered. 'And I spent an hour trying to get back out!'

'A maze?' Eldin frowned. 'What in hell good is that? Are we to spend days without number exploring a maze?'

'The legends tell of a Black Princess, Yath-Lhi of Tyrhhia, who built a mighty underground maze beneath a great desert,' Aminza thoughtfully said. 'At its centre she kept all the treasures of her silver-spired city, and only she knew the way in. When she went in to admire her hoard, or to add to it, she would have her bearers slain as soon as she led them back out through the maze. When she died, her nation died with her – penniless! No one could ever find the maze's centre.'

'I've heard that story,' Hero nodded.

'Do you think,' Eldin grabbed his shoulders, 'that the First Ones did the same thing?'

'It's possible that the Black Princess copied their idea, yes,' Hero answered. 'But that's no guarantee that there's a treasure.'

'But there might be?'

Hero shrugged.

'Right, let's go!' said Eldin, rubbing his hands together, eager now to be up and at it.

'Ropes first,' reminded Aminza, 'and food in case you have trouble finding your way out. Oh, and plenty of chalk . . .'

'Chalk?' Eldin looked puzzled.

'To mark a trail,' Hero sighed. 'Has love robbed you of all your wits, "old man?" '

'Now see here –'

But Hero ignored him. He rubbed his hands in anticipation, turned to Aminza and said: 'Well, then? Come on, let's get busy, busy! The day wears on and we can't stay here forever. And Eldin –'

'Uh?'

'Wear some warm clothes. It's damned cold in there!'

Down below on the vast, boulder-strewn plateau, Aminza stood out from the shadow of the keep and looked up at the men where they toiled upward. They had used the ropes for a quick, safe climb, rather than spend exhausting hours on the job, which had been Hero's lot that very morning. Now it was mid-afternoon, and high on the face of the keep the men looked like spiders to Aminza Anz and their ropes like strands of web.

To them she, too, looked insectlike, and catching sight of her where she stood far below, David Hero glanced speculatively at his burly companion. They had just hauled themselves up onto a narrow ledge and now sat dangling their legs in thin air.

'How old are you, anyway?' queried the younger dreamer, brushing dust and fine debris from his brown trousers.

'Eh? I'm forty-seven. Why do you ask?'

'You still climb very well,' Hero answered, after a moment of thought. 'Especially for one who couldn't draw breath without choking only a handful of weeks ago'

'I always was good on a face,' Eldin preened. 'Perhaps I was a mountaineer in the waking world.' Then he looked shrewdly at his friend. 'But you can't fool me, lad. That's not really why you asked my age, is it? Still, I'll play your game. And how old are you; thirty-two, aren't you?'

Hero nodded. 'Aye, fifteen years your junior. But I was only twenty-six when first we met.'

'And you're wondering how an old lad like Eldin

the Wanderer managed to catch a pretty little butter-
fly like Aminza, eh? And right under your nose, at
that!'

Hero shook his head. 'No, not at all; though I'll
grant you she's a pretty enough creature for any man.
But we've been together now for six years, and –'

'Ah! *Now* I understand,' cried Eldin. 'You think
that this will split us up, right?'

'Oh, it'll do that eventually, no doubt about it –
but,' he shrugged. 'All for the best, really, I suppose . . .' And Hero picked at his square nails and
gazed off into space.

'What?' Eldin scowled. 'What? Are you trying to
tell me something? How do you mean, "all for the
best?"'

'Well, they have a saying in some of the villages
where *I've* lodged,' Hero answered. 'More a poem,
really.' He paused. 'But I don't suppose it applies to
such as us. I mean, after all, we're from the waking
world. You know – foreigners.'

'Foreigners? We're damned dreamers, that's all.
And if one of us *is* a foreigner, why, it's you! You
haven't even earned yourself a dream-name yet!'

'Ah, well,' Hero shrugged. 'Forget it.' He pointed
at a deep shaded crack in the rock face. 'That's it,' he
said. 'The entrance.'

Before Eldin could comment, the younger man
stood up on the precarious ledge, found easy hand-
and footholds overhead and pulled himself leisurely
up and into the fault. They were roped together. Eldin
watched Hero disappear, felt the rope tighten about
his waist and followed. A moment later they stood
together in cool shade, peering into gloom where the
fissure's flat floor receded into the heart of the keep.

'Go on, then,' said Eldin. 'Say it.'

'Eh? Say what?' asked Hero innocently, peering at

the stone floor beneath his feet. 'See here,' he pointed. 'These tracks in the dust here. They're mine. But these others, they can only be Thinistor's. Come on, let's not hang about.' And as their eyes became more accustomed to the dim interior of the keep, so they moved forward.

'Hold!' commanded Eldin before they'd gone more than a dozen paces. Hero looked at him and could see that he was rapidly losing his temper. 'Say your damned saying, or your "poem," or whatever. Say it now, or damn your eyes I'll go no farther!'

Hero sighed. 'You won't like it,' he warned. 'You'll only want to fight.'

'What, me? Fight? Over a silly poem? No, no,' the other vigorously shook his great head. 'Not over a fool's rhyme!'

'Well, anyway, I won't say it,' said Hero, his voice echoing hollowly in the gloomy rock passage. 'We've no time now for fighting.'

'Say it!' roared the other, and they both winced at the echoes that came thundering back.

'Are you trying to bring the whole keep down on our heads?" Hero whispered. 'All right, all *right!* I'll say it:

> "A man's a man till forty,
> But past that, as a rule,
> He's old and rude and naughty,
> And any female's –" '

'Hold!' Eldin snarled. 'Don't you *dare* say it! You just this minute made the damn thing up anyway. Here, let me lead the way.'

'Careful as you go!' cried Hero as the other brushed brusquely by him. 'Easy, I say. Just around that corner there's a –' And he threw himself flat on the dusty floor, wedging his body tight with arms, elbows, head and feet in the narrow corridor.

'– *Pitfall!*' came the cry of the other as his weight fell on the rope, nearly jerking Hero loose. It took Eldin only a moment or two to haul himself back to safety, and when Hero felt the rope slacken he crept round the corner of rock to lie flat beside his friend and peer down into the black depths.

Without a word the younger dreamer took a prepared brand from the pack on his back. He struck flint and flames instantly burst from the torch. The two stared down into the black reaches of an apparently bottomless pit. Hero looked sideways at the older man. The sight of his companion's throat undulating so rapidly as he nervously gulped and swallowed was something one might only witness once or twice in a lifetime. To emphasize a point, Hero plucked a piece of burning rag from the torch and let it fall. For well over a minute the flaring speck of light could be seen receding into unguessed depths before it was swallowed up in darkness.

'A good thing we were tied together,' said Hero.

'Aye,' Eldin readily agreed. 'David –'

'I accept your apology,' the other preempted him.

'Good! And no more needling?'

'And no more bull-headed arguing?'

'And an end to bloody "poetry?" '

'And no dream name-calling!'

They grinned at each other in the flickering torchlight.

'Which way do we go?' Eldin finally asked.

'See there, the ledge along the wall? It's narrow but safe enough.' Hero held his torch high and the shadows were pushed back. The chasm was about twenty-five feet wide and indeed a narrow rim of rock crossed it along one wall.

'I was along there once already, remember? Keep your face to the wall and you'll find handholds galore. Follow me, but quietly. And listen, old Thinistor did us a favour. From here on in he left warnings – probably reminders for himself – smudges of dye in hazardous places. White is safe, red means danger!'

'Fine, but – don't you think that now would be a good time to get rid of this rope? It just saved my life, granted, but next time it might mean the end of both of us.'

'Agreed,' said Hero. 'Only be careful. Remember, I know the way – or at least some of it – and it's a pretty tricky way, you may believe me!'

II
THE KEEP'S CORE

Half an hour later they had reached Hero's previous point of penetration. To do so they had to bypass a further half-dozen fearsome falls, where the floor would have slid away beneath their feet; they had to avoid pivoting slabs of stone which would slam down from the walls if a foot should fall in the wrong place; and they had to tightrope across a great chasm on a bridge of stone which in places was less than six inches in width.

They had received adequate warning of each of these hazards in the shape of Thinistor's smudges of red dye strategically daubed on the walls; but the latest obstacle was one which spoke eloquently if mutely for itself, explaining why Hero had chosen to go no farther on his own.

For now they had come to a place where the floor of the tunnel suddenly fell away vertically to a depth of some eighty feet, but this pit of its own was not what had stopped the younger dreamer. Casting one of his torches into the depths after first lighting a second from its flame, David Hero lighted up the floor of the pit. The torch had fallen speedily, landing with a strangely heavy thump and going out almost immediately, but not before the adventurers had seen the many white bones that littered the pit's bottom – the bones, and the coils of rope on which they lay and with which they were intermingled.

'You can see why I went no farther,' Hero said, holding his torch high to light up the ceiling. 'See there? That thick bar of metal that crosses the ceiling from wall to wall? And do you see the frayed ropes that hang from it? What do you suppose happened here?'

'Hmph!' Eldin grunted. 'Isn't it obvious? Over the years a good many adventurers have found their way in here. They've thrown their ropes up over the bar and attempted to swing across – but their ropes snapped and they fell to their deaths.'

'All of them?'

'Eh? What do you mean?'

'Can you honestly see any adventurer worth his salt trying to swing across there on a weak rope?' Hero shook his head. 'Oh, no. There's something very fishy here. And see, there's old Thinistor's warning on the wall.'

Eldin looked as directed, and sure enough there was the wizard's smudge of warning red. The burly dreamer scowled. 'It's simply his warning of a hazard,' he grunted. 'Just like all the others we've seen.'

'But that's just it,' Hero insisted. 'All of those other hazards were hidden, more or less, but this one is clearly visible. Or is Thinistor warning us of something we can't see?'

'There's a way to find out,' grunted Eldin. 'Here, give me one of those grappling-hooks of yours.'

Hero took an iron hook from his belt and passed it over. Eldin tied the end of a slender but extremely strong rope to the hook, whirled it round his head and expertly released it. The iron soared up and over the bar, was pulled back by Eldin until its tines caught fast. 'There you go,' he said with some satisfaction. 'All ready to swing.'

'As were all the others,' Hero frowned. 'Here, I've an idea. Let's see what happens if –' and he searched the floor around his feet until he found a large, jagged rock, fallen from the ceiling in unknown ages past. Carefully, he cut the rope and tied the rock to its end with a firm knot. Then, with a great push, he sent the weighted rope swinging out over the chasm. Like a pendulum, the stone should have swung away and returned to Hero's hands – but it did not!

At the halfway point, as if caught and pulled from below by the hand of some invisible giant, the rock plummetted downward trailing strands of snapped rope.

What in the name of –?' the dreamers whispered in unison.

Hero found a smaller stone, whipped his hand back, then forward, shot the projectile out across the chasm. Instead of shooting straight across to the other side, the pebble curved sharply downward, accelerated, slammed into the scattering of bones below. It failed to bounce.

Eldin's eyebrows beetled as he lowered them in a frown. 'As the stones approach the centre, so they –'

'– get heavier!' Hero finished it for him. 'And so did our friends down there.' He pointed at the dark depths below, where bones lay scattered in white and shattered disarray. 'When they tried to swing across, they grew too heavy for their ropes!'

'Magic!' Eldin snarled, his fear of the supernatural visible in his wide eyes and bared teeth.

'I don't think so,' said Hero. 'At least, not the sort of magic you mean. This is something the First Ones left behind them.'

'How do you mean?' Eldin asked.

'Well, you know how a northstone always points to the north? I think there's something down there, buried in the heart of the keep, that pulls things into it in much the same way. Except that it pulls harder.'

'Hmph!' Eldin grunted. 'A damned sight harder, I'd say! So how did old Thinistor get across?'

Now it was Hero's turn to frown. 'Let's not forget he was a wizard,' he said.

'Aye, but if this is something the First Ones left behind, surely its power would supersede his?' At times Eldin could display alarming powers of logic.

Hero scratched his head for a moment, then snapped his fingers. 'He walked across!'

'Eh? Walked? Are you feeling well, lad?'

'Across the bottom!' the other sighed. 'He climbed down on a rope, walked across, climbed the other side!'

'And he didn't get heavier on the way down?'

'We can soon find out.' Hero hammered a spike into a crack in the floor, tied a rope to it, tossed the thin coil over the lip. Lying down, he held his torch out over the rim and gazed into the depths. In the flickering torchlight he could just see that the rope had reached bottom.

'What does that prove?' Eldin asked.

'Well,' Hero answered, hauling on the rope which came up easily enough, 'the rope itself hasn't got any heavier, has it? So neither will we when we climb down. I think the pull increases toward the centre. That's where all the bones are.'

'But you can't be sure . . .'

'No, but I'm willing to go first. Here, hold the

torch. When I get to the bottom I'll light another.' And passing Eldin the torch, he grasped the rope and swung himself over the rim and out of sight.

After a while, when the rope went slack, Eldin called out: 'Are you all right, David?'

'Fine!' came the answer. 'Come on down.' And a sudden flaring light from below confirmed Hero's safe arrival at the bottom of the pit.

Eldin immediately threw down his torch and lowered himself over the edge. A minute later he stood beside his younger friend and stared along the length of the pit across the scattered bones at its centre to the sheer wall at the other end. 'Here we go,' said Hero, stepping out gingerly toward that far wall.

Eldin followed and with each step, as they approached the centre of the pit, so they felt weight settling invisibly on their shoulders, their limbs, every part of their bodies. *'Uh!'* said Eldin, 'I feel as if I were carrying three men!'

Hero, ahead by two paces, answered: 'Where I am it feels like five! And look –!' Eldin looked in time to see the flames of his friend's torch dragged *downward* and snuffed out as they crawled along the stock of the torch toward Hero's fingers.

'Those flames,' Hero grunted, 'might just have had the right idea. In fact –' he got down on hands and knees, '– I think I'd better crawl before something snaps!'

Eldin, too, got down on all fours. His very clothes now felt as if they were made of lead; and the bones of the pit, as he pushed them out of his way, were heavy as boulders. Now the dreamers were panting, sucking at air which seemed compressed and hard as iron. Literally wriggling forward on their bellies, they dragged their chins in the dust and bones, cutting knees and elbows as their weight became that of ten men and more.

'Whatever you do, don't stop!' Hero gasped. 'Or you'll be here forever.' Then, silent except for their panting, gasping, wriggling and clawing, they gave their all to fighting their way out of this region of monstrous magnetism.

After what seemed like hours, finally they could get back onto all fours, and moments later climb weakly to their feet, until at last they leaned on trembling legs against the sheer wall of rock at the far side of the pit.

'I could sleep for a week,' Eldin sighed while Hero lit a torch.

'Me, too,' the other agreed, '– which is all the more reason to get moving again. We'll climb this face, take a bite to eat and a quick swig of water, and press on immediately. I've a feeling there's not much farther to go.'

'To what?'

'To whatever it was kept old Thinistor up here in the Great Bleak Mountains all these years,' Hero answered. He handed Eldin the torch, attached a small grappling-hook to a coil of light, strong rope, whirled the hook round his head and let it fly up and over the rim of the looming wall. At their feet, the coil of rope unwound itself with a hiss, and moments later –

They began to hop about and yelp, covering their heads with their arms as the rope fell back in loose loops and the hook came clattering down out of darkness. It missed Eldin by inches and Hero caught it on the bounce.

'If at first you don't succeed –' Hero muttered in what he hoped was a placating tone; but Eldin simply snatched the hook from him and scowled blackly.

'Here, you hold the torch,' he snarled. 'I'm damned if I'll stand here and be pounded to death by ill-tossed grappling-irons!' With a great heave, he shot the hook into the air. It caught at once and he gave a jerk on the rope, sinking the hook into the floor of the passage eighty feet above. 'There!' he said with satisfaction. 'Now you can climb.'

'After you,' said Hero promptly. 'You're heavier than I am. You go first and anchor the rope for me.'

'Oh? And what if it slips when I'm half-way up?'

Hero shrugged. 'You threw it,' he blandly replied.

With a snort and an oath Eldin gave the rope a second tug, then grunted as he braced his legs against the wall and started to climb. Hero watched him in open admiration, and in less than two minutes was able to follow on when the older man called down to him and announced his safe arrival at the top . . .

After hauling up the rope the pair sat down on the cold stone floor, ate some dried meat and drank a little water; but while Eldin would have been content to rest a while longer, his younger companion was eager to push on. 'Come on,' Hero said, getting stiffly to his feet. 'The sooner we've done with this the better. We're low on ropes, irons and torches, and our food and water's not much to mention. I'd hate to get stuck in here.'

'I suppose so,' the other grudgingly agreed. 'But look, what's that up ahead?' The both stared into the darkness ahead, a darkness partly illuminated by the flickering light of their torch, which seemed reflected now by some vast and polished surface.

As they moved forward so the glow grew brighter, until indeed they could see that the tunnel was sealed by a great plate of shining metal that extended from ceiling to floor and wall to wall. It was inscribed with glyphs utterly alien to the eyes of the adventurers; and yet it seemed to them that there were elements of all dreamland's writings and hieroglyphics hidden in these cryptical etchings of the First Ones.

Greatly daring, Eldin stepped forward and banged on the metal door – for that was surely what the great plate was – with a heavy fist. The door shed clouds of dust and *gonged* hollowly, setting up echoes that reverberated for a long time in the confines of the passage.

Meanwhile Hero was peering at the walls and muttering ominously at something he found there. 'What's wrong now, lad?' Eldin rumbled. 'More of Thinistor's red paint?'

'Red, yes,' Hero answered. '*And* white! The contrary old . . . wizard! How are we to read that?'

'Why, we're to go on!' cried Eldin, '– but carefully!'

'Which means that there has to be a way in,' the younger dreamer grunted, 'if only we can find it.'

'See the crack in the walls, floor and ceiling?' said Eldin. 'The door doesn't just block this corridor – it extends *into* the very rock!'

'A sliding door?' Hero asked.

'Perhaps. Or maybe one that opens inward,' the other replied. 'Well, then, if we can't *push* it open –' and they leaned their shoulders mightily against it, '– perhaps we can slide it to one side, *uh!*' and they tried that too. But the door would not budge.

They sat down in the dust and shared a sip of water; and as Eldin munched morosely on a piece of dried meat, so Hero rapped facetiously on the door and cried: 'Open up in there! I, David Hero, command it!'

And with a hiss and a rumble the great silver panel

instantly slid up into the ceiling, leaving the two comrades to spring to their feet in a blinding blaze of light that spilled like the fires in the heart of the sun out from beyond the raised portal.

'This is it,' Hero cried, crouching down and shielding his eyes from the awesome glare. 'We've done it. We've reached the core of the keep!'

III
THE KEEPER

As Hero strode forward into the glare from the open door, so Eldin grabbed him by the back of his brown jacket, bringing him to an abrupt halt. 'Easy, lad. We don't know what's in there – yet!'

'Knowledge, old friend,' Hero answered. 'Or treasure, perhaps. All your heart desires. No, we don't know what's in there – but whatever it is, old Thinistor was mighty keen for it.'

'Aminza reckons he was only after power: the power of the First Ones!'

'Maybe he was, and maybe he wasn't. We'll never know if we stay out here. And look, now that the dazzles's faded a bit, why, there's nothing at all in there to be afraid of!'

'Afraid?' Eldin stiffened. 'Did you think I was afraid?' He released his grip on Hero's jacket. 'Who, me? Afraid of a few bright lights glaring at us out of this lair of the First Ones? Of all those shiny things I can see in there? Of metal doors that slide up into the ceiling and disappear? Afraid? . . . Damned *right* I am! You go first.' And he gave Hero a push in the middle of his back.

The younger dreamer staggered forward, his curved blade whispering from its sheath where he had strapped it behind his back for ease in climbing.

113

Eldin, too, unsheathed his sword, covering the back of his colleague. They crossed the threshold –

– And behind them the door gave a *hiss* and slid down out of the ceiling!

Sensing the door's descent even as it moved, the two turned and sprang for the opening all in one movement. Both of them bounced off the still shivering metal panel and fell, crouching, to face one another.

'Wonderful!' Eldin snarled, his scarred forehead wrinkling like old leather.

Hero shook himself. He stood up straight and aloof, held out a restraining hand to Eldin, leaned casually against the door, rapped upon it as before and said: 'All right, whoever you are, open up at once!'

'NO!' came a booming, throbbing, echoing answer that had both of the dreamers dropping their swords and clapping hands to ears which rang like the clappers of great bells. *'WHO DARES COMMAND THE KEEPER?'*

Still reeling from the effects of the vast voice's refusal, the two were almost stunned by its question. Stumbling to and fro, they held tightly to ears whose drums felt ruptured, gasping in agonies of sheer, unbearable sound!

'WELL?' the voice slammed at them yet again. *'ARE YOU DUMB?'*

'No!' howled Hero, 'we're not dumb – but we'll damn soon be deaf if you don't lower your voice!'

'Who speaks?' asked the voice again, in a tone mercifully lowered by many decibels.

'I do,' said Hero, retrieving his sword. 'I, David Hero, adventurer in dreams, man of the waking world, keep-climber and swordsmaster – I speak!' He whipped his curved blade through the air, making it sing. 'To whom do I speak?'

'To the Keeper! Who is the other man?'

'I speak for myself,' Eldin rumbled. 'I'm Eldin the Wanderer, dreamer, adventurer and swordsmaster, just like my young friend here – and I eat lesser men for breakfast!'

'*A pair of wanderers, then,*' said the great voice, '*strays from the waking world – and one a cannibal!*'

'He doesn't really eat men,' Hero was quick to point out. 'That was merely an indication of his great strength and skill at arms.'

During their brief conversation with the as yet unseen Keeper, the two intruders had been studying their surroundings. Now that their eyes were accustomed to the brightness and glare of the place, they could see that they stood in a great circular chamber whose walls, like the door, seemed made of some strange silver metal. The floor was padded and springy, with a warmth they could feel through to the soles of their feet, and the ceiling was high and domed. Set in the inward curving walls were huge mirrors (or so these screens appeared to the pair), some of which did in fact mirror their forms; but the surfaces of a greater number were of opaque, misty-grey.

Metal and glass machines and instruments were everywhere, motionless, bright and glittering, but of course the dreamers did not know what they were or how they functioned, or even if they had any functions at all. Ten padded chairs formed a ring about a tall, central hump of metal studded with smaller screens, levers, dials and buttons; but naturally this huge instrument panel was likewise a thing of complete mystery to David Hero and Eldin the Wanderer. They did wonder, however, at the size and odd design of the chairs, and they stood in awe of the minds which could have conceived of and constructed such a place.

Moving carefully around the huge control-center, the two eventually reached a point where they could see its far side. There the screens were alive with small dancing lights and colours, and when the Keeper spoke again they noticed that the patterns of coloured lights seemed to move in rhythm with his voice.

'*You, David Hero: stand on the grey disk, beneath the wheel of globes.*'

Quickly Hero's eyes found the circular plate of grey metal set in the floor. Above it, suspended from the inward-curving ceiling, a wheel-like affair whose spokes terminated in large golden knobs glittered and winked in the changing patterns of light as the echoes of the Keeper's voice died away. Hero was immediately suspicious.

'Why must –' he began, but no sooner had he opened his mouth than a beam of green fire, stabbing from nowhere, singed the hairs on his naked forearms in the nearness of its passing.

'*Do NOT question the Keeper!*' the great voice warned. '*Merely do as I say. No harm will come to you if you obey.*'

With a low-muttered oath and the short hairs of his neck stiffly abristle, the young man stepped gingerly forward and onto the grey disk.

'*Do not be afraid of the lights or the movement of the wheel. I merely wish to look at you,*' came the Keeper's voice, preceding a rapid rotation of the wheel of globes and a silvery haze that sprang downward from its circumference to the grey metal plate, completely enclosing Hero in a tube of light through which his form glowed like a pale pearl.

To Eldin it seemed that his companion was frozen in the tube of light, motionless, and in another moment that he stood in dire peril of his very life! For now Hero's outer form had grown insubstantial as air,

116

while all of his bones and inner organs became clearly visible to Eldin's unbelieving eyes. Obviously, Eldin thought, the silvery haze *was* the Keeper himself – and damn him, he was devouring Hero alive!

In a blur of motion the older man whirled his sword once, twice about his head – and released it straight at the spinning wheel of globes overhead. The sword struck – and disappeared in a blinding flash of light! Tiny pellets of hot metal filled the air, stinging like wasps where they struck and stuck to flesh, and Eldin danced for a moment or two until he had shaken these revenants of his sadly defunct sword from his person.

'FOOL!' cried the Keeper. *'I said he would not be harmed!'* The wheel of golden globes stopped spinning; the silvery haze retracted upward from the grey metal plate; and there stood Hero, unharmed, frowning puzzledly as he noted the dumbfounded expression on his burly friend's face. Before Hero could speak, however, the Keeper said: *'Now your turn, Eldin the Wanderer – and please, no more heroics!'*

Feeling naked without his sword, Eldin stepped awkwardly forward and took Hero's place on the grey plate. Now the younger dreamer watched a repeat performance of what had gone before, and he was similarly alarmed at the sight of Eldin's innards displayed as if his flesh was become water. Since he himself had survived the examination, however, he merely waited until the thing was done and Eldin stepped with a glad sigh of relief from the metal disk back onto the springy, now familiar surface of the floor.

'So, you are what you say you are,' said the Keeper. *'Men of the waking world, and remarkably robust specimens at that. Your race has changed little in a million years. A certain enlargement of the cranium, perhaps, to accommodate larger brains. The discovery of certain scientific techniques, such as the forging of*

117

metals. These and one or two other achievements – and what of writing? Do you know how to use runes or glyphs?'

'There's nothing wrong with our brains!' cried Eldin. 'And we've been forging swords for hundreds of years. As for writing: of course we know its use. Why, in the waking world I was something of a scholar . . . I think. Yes, and we know the runes of dreamland, too.'

'And you, David Hero? Are you so clever?'

'More so,' Hero answered at once. 'I've learned all of dream's runes – almost.'

'He sings, too,' offered Eldin a little peevishly. 'And he makes up poetry. Indeed, with all that learning cramming his cranium, it's a wonder he can think at all!'

'You interest me,' said the still unseen Keeper. *'Yes, I am greatly interested. Sit down in two of the chairs there and be at ease. We shall talk for a while. But a warning: do not touch the instruments on the panels before you. To do so might mean placing your very lives in jeopardy!'*

The two sat, as bidden, if a trifle timidly, but in no time at all they felt soothed by the shifting lights of the panels and eased as the padding of the chairs molded to their forms. 'The First Ones lived in style, eh, Eldin?' said Hero.

'They did that, lad,' came the rumbling reply. 'Maybe that's why they died out: too much soft living.'

'They did not die out,' said the Keeper. *'They merely went away – most of them.'*

'But not all of them,' Hero mused. 'Are you a First One, Keeper?'

'Not I. I merely worked for them.'

'Then they were your masters. And are your masters still here?'

'*They are. Nine of them.*'

'Nine First Ones for ten chairs?' Hero thoughtfully replied.

'*There were ten – once,*' the Keeper answered. '*But enough of this, now I wish to know about you two. Start at that point which first set your feet on the trail that brought you here to the Keep of the First Ones. Leave nothing out, I would know it all. Then, depending on how I judge your tale, I may have work for you.*'

'Work?' growled Eldin. 'We don't sell our swords cheaply, Keeper.'

'*You for one, Eldin the Wanderer, at present have no sword to sell!*' came the immediate response. '*But be sure you would be well repaid for any services rendered.*'

'How repaid?' Hero asked.

'*With riches beyond your wildest dreams,*' came the answer. '*With powers which would make you great in all the dreamlands. With whatever your hearts desire!*'

The two adventurers stared at each other for a moment with shining eyes. Then: 'Shall you begin, or shall I?' asked Eldin of Hero.

Hero cleared his throat. 'We had come down into Theelys . . .' he started.

IV
THE KEEPER'S TALE

'. . . And that's the whole story,' said Eldin with finality. He had taken up the tale's telling when Hero flagged.

For a long moment there was silence and the two dreamers sat patiently and waited for the Keeper to speak. They had grown to associate his voice with the moving lights on a certain panel, so that to them the panel had become the Keeper. During the telling of their story the lights had not been particularly active, but now they flashed and shifted, their moving colours forming intricate and meaningless patterns.

Finally, in a burst of light, the Keeper said: *'Yes, I believe you two will do very nicely. But will you accept the challenge? You worked for Ebraim Borak –'*

'And got not a button out of it,' groused Eldin

'– But you will work for me? For the Great Ones?'

'We did get something out of the Ossaran,' Hero contradicted Eldin. 'We had a good time at his expense in Theelys, and we're not broke yet by a long shot.' To the Keeper, he said: 'We don't have to work for you, you know.'

'True enough, but that would be a very unfortunate matter. Indeed it would.'

'A threat, Keeper?' Eldin questioned, frowning.

'You got into the keep,' the Keeper answered, *'but who is to say you'd get out again?'*

'Definitely a threat,' Hero sighed. 'But what good would it do you to kill us, Keeper?'

'Oh, I would not kill you,' replied the Keeper. *'You would die by no action of mine. No, for that would be against all the Laws. I would simply fail to help you to stay alive. If, as of this moment, I ignored your presence here, then you would never get out. You could not open the door!'*

Hero and Eldin glanced at each other and pulled wry faces.

'As to what good that would do,' the Keeper continued, *'none at all – for you. For me: I would not have to suffer the veritable tribe of wizards and adventurers which your loose tongues would doubtless send here.'*

'We'd not say a word!' cried Eldin in a hurt voice.

'Not until the next time you were drunk,' the Keeper shrewdly answered.

'Huh!' the older dreamer grumbled.

'All right, Keeper, you have the advantage,' Hero grudgingly admitted. 'But we can't very well work for you if we don't know what the work's to be. We've told you our story – now how about you telling us yours?'

Coloured lights flashed as the Keeper considered. Then:

'It would not be my story but the story of the First Ones. But I can see no harm in it, since if you do not accept the quest you will never leave the keep alive! Very well, stay still and listen to the tale . . .

'At the Dawn of Time, many millions of years ago, there was born in the waking world the primal continent of Theem'hdra. No trace of that land and its civilizations has survived the ages, and the greatest savants of Earth do not even admit the possibility of its prehistoric existence. Yet Theem'hdra was. Its

cities teemed with mankind's thronging races and its mountains and forests were alive with strange birds and beasts. And it was man's lot – even the lot of those first men – to live two lives; one in the so-called "waking" world, and the other in the dreamlands. The first gaunts dwelt in Theem'hdra, and so when the first men dreamed, gaunts were borne into dreamland.

'For when all is said and done, dream is only a world lying parallel to the conscious lands of Man, and there are many such parallel worlds. And so intelligent men lived in Theem'hdra and dreamed their first dreams, and life came to the dreamlands; and they were powerful dreamers, some of those early men. The architecture of Theem'hdra lives on in some of dreamland's cities even now, notably Inquanok, for the Northmen of the primal continent were cold and hard and their cities likewise. And Inquanok will last as long as dreams themselves . . .

'And across all the mighty distances of space there was life, and life was scattered down the timestreams, its diverse forms like many-coloured grains of sand strewn throughout the limitless space-time universe of planets and places and parallel worlds.

'The race of the First Ones was old even then, but not the oldest of races by any means. They called themselves the First Ones because they thought they were, and when they discovered even older races – well, still they kept their old name. Perhaps it was vanity, or perhaps that was simply the name by which they had come to be known.

'And the First Ones discovered many marvels. Their savants were masters of science and sorcery, who plumbed the voids betwixt stars and times and the misted mysteries of parallel planes of existence. They made a great study of all intelligent forms of life; and eventually they came to Theem'hdra, where already Man had risen up from his pre-dawn ancestors. There they established their great keeps in the Mighty Circle Mountains – just as here in dreamland they have set them in the Great Bleak Range – and from the keeps they went out in clever disguises to study the ways of Man.

'Then it was that they discovered mention in the myths and legends of Man of those eternally damned demon gods of the Cthulhu Cycle, which seeped down out of the stars in Earth's earliest days and built their hideous titan cities in the steaming fens of the dawn-world. And such were these legends that they fascinated the First Ones, for according to writings predating Earthly life Cthulhu and certain of his cohorts yet lived on, prisoned in hidden places and sending visions to the minds of men which turned their dreams to nightmares. And so the legends concerning the Cthulhu Cycle had extended into the dreamlands, where revenant nightmares nurtured seeds of an elder horror and the mad dreams of Cthulhu wandered abroad, ever ready to seize upon the dreaming minds of mortal men.

'Ah! And when the First Ones sought to ascertain the truth of the olden myths – whether or not Cthulhu and certain of his contemporaries indeed lived on – then they recoiled in horror from that which they discovered: namely that the legends lied not! Cthulhu lived – he lives! – and he will never cease in his efforts to free himself from magic-forged chains and roam free again in the sane and ordered universe, breeding madness and ruin and horror and chaos!

'Then the First Ones pursued Cthulhu's legends no longer but turned themselves to the task of reinforcing the immemorial prisons of the terrible *demon gods. And again they discovered their vanity shaken, for to admit that Cthulhu and his spawn were prisoned was to admit that some even mightier Beings had prisoned them: and thus the First Ones would fathom the secrets of the great Elder Gods, whose home is called Elysia.*

'And for the first time the First Ones found themselves denied access to a place or time or parallel world, for such was the might of the great Elder Gods that they had built Elysia and hidden it away where it might never be found or visited or even suspected by anyone or thing which had not the right so to find, visit or suspect it. And so the First Ones gave up their efforts to seek out the Elder Gods, and they wisely withdrew from any further tampering or discovery or even curiosity concerning the natures or manner of being of the immemorially prisoned demon gods of the Cthulhu Cycle.

'Of the terrible demon gods themselves: suffice to say that Yibb-Tstll – of whom you now have some knowledge, since you have met and dealt with one of his many avatars – is one of the lesser demon gods. The others are . . . they are much worse!

'But to continue:

'And so the First Ones completed their studies of early civilized man, and of other life-forms in that area of the space-time universe, and moved back into the keeps to prepare them for a move to some new and hitherto unexplored region. Now the keeps had stood in the waking world for thousands of years, so that the men of the primal continent of Theem'hdra no longer remembered anything but the vaguest of legends concerning their coming; and when they left – ah! – that was a marvellous thing: these massive cubes of centuries-weathered stone levering themselves loose from the earth and flying off across the

world to disappear into strange times and stranger
dimensions.

'Here in the dreamlands, however . . .' (and here
the two dreamers sensed a sort of wry shrug in the
voice of the Keeper, though none was visible except
perhaps in a momentary flickering of coloured lights)
'. . . here, all was not well. There were three keeps in
the dreamlands, and the First Ones who controlled
them were to take their leave of men's dreams soon
after the exodus of their fellows from Theem'hdra.
The time of their leaving the dreamlands was not
important, for time is different here; and anyway,
these three keeps were not accompanying the greater
force but intended to journey to the dreamlands of
other worlds. Alas, it was not to be.*

'One of the First Ones – wrong-headed and wilful,
a renowned lover of mysteries and Explorer of
Unknowns without peer – defied the decision of the
Council of First Ones and secretly sought out Cthulhu
and others of his ilk here in the dreamlands. Aye, and
having found what he sought his payment was perma-
nent madness! Deranged, he became a minion of
Cthulhu and set out to perform certain tasks for that
great demon god.*

'Firstly, he stole from one of the keeps – this very
keep whose Keeper speaks to you – the three Wands
of Power, one of which eventually fell into Thinistor
Udd's hands and now lies in his temple-cave. Without
that wand and its lost companions, the remaining nine
masters of the keep (aye, for the Cthulhu-maddened
First One is indeed the missing tenth member of the
keep's crew) became marooned here in your dreamland. For the wands control the greater force which
powers the keep on its long voyages between the stars.*

'Secondly, the deranged First One, Klarek-Yam by
name, caused those things to happen which destroyed

*utterly the inhabitants of the other keeps. It was
thought that he would try to do the same to his own
keep, but something must have happened to him all
those many aeons agone to foil his mad design. Then,
because my remaining nine masters could no longer
leave earth's dreamland, and since they had no desire
to live out their lives here, they placed themselves in a
deep sleep until the time should come when the wands
might be returned. They remain asleep to this day,
and still the wands have not been returned.*

*'The First Ones are not immortal, you see, though
they are exceedingly long-lived; and so they must con-
serve their lives by suspending them in the sleep, during which they do not age. And so they sleep, hidden
away within this very keep, dreaming dreams within
dreams as they wait for their hoped for but long-
delayed release . . .'*

'Much like Cthulhu and his spawn, from what
you've been telling us,' Eldin rumbled; and Hero
thought to himself: 'How clever of the old lad!'

Clever or not, the Keeper seemed offended. *'Do
you dare compare my good and kind masters to the
filthy, crawling spawn of Cthulhu?'*

'Your good, kind, weak masters,' said David Hero,
with the emphasis on weak.

'WHAT? "WEAK," DID YOU SAY?'

'Calm down, calm down,' answered the younger
dreamer placatingly. 'Surely you can see, Keeper,
that's the way it looks? Why did the nine not go out
and find the tenth for themselves, recovering the
wands and so assuring their safe departure from these
regions? Did they think that going to sleep – even a
long, long sleep – was going to solve all their problems for them?'

'But Klarek-Yam had the Wands of Power!' the
Keeper blusteringly replied. *'Against weapons such as*

the wands, how could my masters hope to prevail?'

'Y'know,' rumbled Eldin the Wanderer, 'I think Hero's right. Why don't you wake up the nine and let them go find the wands themselves? After all, this Klarek-Yam must be aeons-dead by now.'

'When the First Ones wish to be awakened, then shall I awaken them. They have indicated no such desire. No, there is a better way.'

'And we're it,' said Hero with a sigh. 'Right?'

'Correct. Using the first wand, you shall seek out the others and return them to the keep.'

'And how might we use the first wand when we can't even touch the damned thing?' Eldin roared. 'Haven't we already explained that?'

Now it was the Keeper's turn to be placating. *'Calm, calm,'* he said. *'You shall see what you shall see. Now then, gather up all the small pieces of metal which once were your sword, Eldin. And Hero, you help him.'*

Muttering, the dreamers obeyed, collecting the fused fragments of Eldin's blade and placing them on a large handkerchief laid out on the floor. When they had gathered together all that they could find, the Keeper said:

'Now place the sundered, melted bits of sword on the grey metal plate where you stood for your examination. Good! Now stand back, well back.'

The dreamers obeyed and once more the wheel of globes began to spin. This time the hazy tube which sprang from ceiling to floor was of a golden hue which turned the room a glowing yellow. In less than a minute the job was done and Eldin's sword, reconstituted, lay on the grey metal plate shinier and newer than ever before the dreamers had beheld it.

Grumbling to himself to cover his amazement, Eldin advanced and retrieved his blade. 'It seems to be lighter,' he said, swishing the sword through the air.

'You must have missed some of the bits,' replied the Keeper, *'but I assure you that the sword is stronger than ever it was. Also, it is now filled with the aura of the First Ones. Only touch Thinistor Udd's wand with that sword, and the wand will give you no more trouble.'*

'Oh?' Eldin seemed doubtful.

'Indeed. And now you must be about the quest.'

'We haven't said we'll do it yet,' reminded Hero.

'But you will.' The Keeper's voice seemed to chuckle.

'What's to stop us agreeing to your quest?' Eldin queried, 'and then, when we're free of the keep, going our own way?' And he nimbly side-stepped Hero's swift dig at his ribs.

'Very little, it would seem,' the Keeper replied; then continued: *'Now listen. When you have Thinistor's wand, simply dangle it from a thread, like a north-stone, and it will point out the quickest route to the second wand. When you have acquired the second wand, then matters will take their own course.'*

'And is that all?' asked Hero when it appeared that the Keeper was through speaking.

'It is. Only remember to return the Wands of Power to the keep when all is done. What could be easier?' His voice faded away and the lights began slowly to dim. In another moment the massive silver door hissed up into the ceiling and the exit lay open to the gaze of the two dreamers.

Without more ado, as the lights further dimmed and began to go out, they made their exit.

PART FOUR

PART FOUR

I

THE DESCENT

Early morning sunshine covered the plateau and made long brown shadows. The three adventurers were outside the entrance to the late Thinistor Udd's cave, their necessaries split into three packs: two fairly large ones, and one much smaller for Aminza. Eldin the Wanderer sat on a rock, tenderly examining a naked arm where he had rolled up the sleeve of his jacket.

'What in all the dreamlands are you so sore about?' David Hero spoke to the older dreamer. 'What are a few hairs to a walking doormat like you?'

'A few hairs, he says – a few!' Eldin rumbled volcanically. 'Hell's bells, lad – the damned thing nearly singed my arm off! "Only touch the wizard's wand with your sword," says the Keeper. And like a damned fool – I did!'

Hero grinned as he slitted his eyes against the sun and peered at Eldin's hairless arm. 'Well, he was right, wasn't he? We've had no more trouble, have we? Your sword drew the wand's last blast and that was that. And look!' and he held up a length of twine with the wand suspended at its end.

'And it works, too,' said Aminza. 'See how it points the way . . .'

'Well, er, yes,' said Hero, somewhat less happily.

'But there might be something a little wrong there. I mean, the damn thing's pointing north!' Sure enough, the wand's knob not only pointed north but was actually tilted upward – up the final slope to the spot where Eldin and Hero had confronted the demon god Yibb-Tstll.

' "Something's a little wrong there!" ' mimicked Eldin, rolling down his sleeve. 'I'll say there is. Just over that final ridge there's a damn great cliff that looks like it goes down to dreamland's core! And that's our quickest route to the next wand, is it? Well, I say we head for Theelys. Ebraim Borak owes us a deal of money – and I owe him a couple of broken ribs at least.'

'Was that cliff really unclimbable?' Aminza asked of the two men.

'Can't really say,' mused Hero. 'It looked a bit tough, I'll admit, but remember I wasn't looking at it from a very comfortable angle. And there again, a lot of things are a far sight easier in dreams.'

'That's as it may be,' Eldin rumbled, 'but they can be a damn sight harder, too. I'll grant you one thing, though: there's never been anything easier than falling off a cliff!'

'Hmm,' frowned Hero, his eyes following the knob of the wand where it aimed itself at the rocky ridge. He twirled it once or twice at the end of its twine, but each time he did so the wand quickly steadied to its previous position, and always it pointed to the ridge.

'Well,' said Aminza, 'what's it to be? Or are we going to stay here forever?'

'You're a plucky lass, Aminza,' said Hero with feeling, 'but I reckon Eldin's right. If it was just the two of us, perhaps we'd give it a try. But with you along . . . it's a tough climb, sure enough.'

'It's Theelys, then?' she said.

'Looks that way,' Eldin rumbled, climbing to his feet, disappointment clearly audible in his voice. They shouldered their packs and turned south. 'Since we already know the way,' the older dreamer continued, 'I suppose we'd do well simply to retrace our route. What do you say, Hero?'

'Eh?' the younger dreamer tugged distractedly at the wand, frowned, then let go of the thing and stepped back in amazement. Suspended in midair, floating free and dangling its thread beneath it, the wand hovered four feet above the rocky ground and stubbornly pointed north, up the steep slope to the ultimate crest.

'Well I'll be –' Hero started, gritting his teeth and taking both hands to the wand. Strain as he might the wand would not budge. As soon as Hero took a pace or two up the slope, however, then the wand went along meekly enough.

'– A monkey's uncle!' gasped Eldin, putting the finishing touch to his friend's incomplete comment. 'Well, here's a fine thing. We won't go north and the wand won't come south. What now?'

'We could leave it here . . .' suggested Aminza.

'We'll get nothing else out of Ebraim Borak if we do,' said Hero.

'Except a deal of satisfaction when I break his arm,' growled Eldin.

'Or . . .' the girl said, and waited for a response from her friends from the waking world.

'Are we to come out of this utterly empty-handed?' asked Hero, jutting his chin aggressively.

'With nothing but a few tonds between us?' added Eldin.

The three formed a triangle about the wand where it pointed up the slope and quivered like a dog on a leash. Hero licked his lips. 'All our hearts could ever desire, the Keeper said.'

'And a fine, adventurous quest in the bargain,' Eldin rumbled.

Aminza stamped her little foot and laughed. 'Why, it couldn't have worked out better if you'd planned it this way!' she cried.

The two men peered at each other and grinned wolfishly. 'What's life without a taste of danger now and then?' asked Eldin.

Hero sucked a finger and held it up, testing the wind. 'North it is,' he said, and they turned their faces up the slope.

Up until now the cliff face had not been too difficult, though difficult enough, and the climbers had made good use of the weathered face's many hand- and footholds where the sun's warmth had dried them out. The summit had long since disappeared into a mist-hazed sky and in places the cliff was concave, which meant that the three must remain securely roped together for long periods. Aminza had proved to be a good, natural climber, which helped matters, but Hero and Eldin could have progressed a lot faster on their own. Now they had found themselves a wide ledge on which to rest, and Eldin had brewed a pot of tea.

'I'm so tired,' said Aminza, stretching her body to ease its aches and pains.

'It's the climbing,' Eldin rumbled. 'It gets you that way when you're not used to it.' To Hero he said: 'How deep are we, do you think?'

Hero shrugged. He gazed out and down into deeps which were grey and swirling, full of heaving vapours. 'Look at it down there. You'd almost believe you could walk on it. And it seems to get thicker the deeper we go. As to how deep we are – we could be deeper,' he answered a trifle grudgingly. 'We've come down maybe six, seven thousand feet, but it must be well into the afternoon by now. We can only go half as far on the next leg, for then Aminza will be exhausted. Which means that if we don't strike bottom in the next three hours or so –'

'We'll be stuck on the cliff face for the night,' said Aminza with a shudder. 'And it's all my fault.'

'Not at all, my dear,' Eldin gently rumbled, placing an arm about her shoulders where they sat dangling their feet in empty air. 'Don't blame yourself, lass, for we all knew what we were doing when we set out. And anyway, it won't be the first time Hero and I have faced nightfall on the face of a cliff. We'll make out all right.'

'Providing it doesn't rain,' said Hero. 'And there are no visits from stray gaunts. And no rock falls . . .' and he glanced ominously upward.

Aminza began quietly to snivel a little and Eldin glared at Hero where he leaned his back against the cliff. Hero cast his eyes to the heavens, gritted his teeth and silently tut-tutted for a moment, then said:

'Eldin's right. Don't blame yourself, Aminza. It's not every girl could have done half so well. Now sip your tea and take it easy. We'll rest ourselves here for a half-hour or so, then carry on down. If only it wasn't so misty down there, we might be able to see the bottom. At least the wand doesn't seem to have any doubts. Look –' And he dangled the wand from its thread and showed how it pointed northward into space and slightly downward into the ever-thickening mists below.

'Somewhere down there,' Hero nodded in the direction the wand pointed, 'we'll find the second wand – eventually.'

'Umm,' said Eldin. 'Well, for the immediate future I'll be happy simply to get down off this damned cliff.

In the meantime – break out a piece of meat, eh, David? Let's have something to chew on . . .'

Half an hour later they set off again and at first the going was a lot easier. They followed a route which moved to the left as it descended, and there were plenty of hand- and footholds. After about an hour, however, they began to hear the rush of water and the rock of the face rapidly grew slimy.

'The very last of the thaw,' grunted Eldin, examining the smooth knob of a huge boulder which stuck out from the cliff's face.

Close behind him, Hero said: 'Yes, and it's not only making the going nasty but thickening the mist, too.' Turning his head to look back, he said, 'Are you all right, girl?'

Aminza nodded, her face shiny and damp as the rocks. She bravely tried a smile but it didn't quite come off. Her arms felt like lead and she just couldn't seem to draw air quickly enough. 'I'm fine,' she gasped.

Meanwhile Eldin had embraced the great boulder which blocked his way. With his huge arms wrapped about it, slowly he slid his chest over its surface toward the far side. There the narrow ledge they had been following continued its steep downward route. When he was safely across he moved on a pace or two until he could see around a sharp corner in the face of the cliff.

'We're in trouble now,' he groaned, 'and that's for sure.'

'What's up?' Hero queried, stretching himself to the limit to embrace the great round rock. A moment later he was beside Eldin and they peered together in silent dismay at the scene that awaited them beyond the corner of the cliff.

It was a great waterfall, and its rush was a tumult of sound now that the cliff's face no longer protected their ears. Below, the mists boiled and tossed; the rock ahead was sheer and glistened slickly. It looked utterly impossible. And yet . . .

As Hero's ears became used to the roar of the cataract he began to grin. 'Listen,' he shouted above the roaring of falling water. 'Do you hear it?'

'Hear what?' cried Eldin in return.

'Why, the water striking bottom!' Hero shouted back. 'We've almost made it. If we go back a little way and take a different route, we should be down within minutes. At worst we should find ourselves on a different sort of face; a slope, perhaps, at the bottom of the cliff.'

Grinning, the two looked back along the ledge.

Three or four paces away Aminza was clambering over the great boulder that blocked her path. She had not the reach in her arms to skirt the rock in the manner of her friends. Even as the two watched her, they saw the boulder tilt outward from the cliff. Its hold weakened by the steady seep of moisture, the great rock was unable to take her weight.

'Aminza!' Eldin croaked – and a split second later she gave a little shriek as the boulder tilted farther yet and seemed almost to shrug her into space. For an instant it was as if she floated gently downward – before her plummeting weight snatched first Hero, then Eldin from the slippery ledge.

Tied together they fell, a giant bolas whirling in air. Mist sucked their rushing bodies in, savoured them, coughed them out onto a surface resilient as water.

It *was* water! A deep, cold lake.

Deep they sank, then fought weakly for the surface.

Gasping as they bobbed like corks in a froth of wavelets, they saw first the sheer wall of rock going up into mist, then, to their right, a tiny shingle bay luxuriant with tall, fernlike trees.

They swam, and in a matter of minutes which seemed like hours felt the sloping bottom beneath their weary feet. Still roped together they dragged themselves up onto the pebbly beach. And there they lay for some time, drinking deep of the damp air and thanking their lucky stars that they yet lived . . .

II
WHIRLPOOL!

Between the nodding trees, far down on the beach, Aminza could see her friends from the waking world where they worked, naked except for tiny loincloths, lashing together a raft from fallen trunks of the giant, hollow, reedy trees. Back here in the cave they had found, overhung by the mighty cliff and protected from the dank air by thick foliage, she dried out their clothes before a roaring fire and watched the two as they struggled, mist-wreathed, lashing trunks together with tough, rubbery vines.

They had been at it for hours now, and must surely be worn out, but still they struggled on. Their clothes were almost dry and Aminza, completely naked, wanted to be dressed before the men had finished their raft. She watched their activity for a while longer, then tried her clothes for dryness yet again.

She had long since given up the flimsy garments which Thinistor Udd had made her wear – had done so before the decision had been taken to set out upon this present quest – and now her clothes were of much the same cut as those of her companions. She had found them in one of Thinistor's storage caves, and doubtless they had belonged to some small adventurer sent into the mountains by Ebraim Borak, but Aminza did not like to think on the fate of their previous owner. As she dressed herself she was pleased that the soft leather of her jacket and short trousers in no way disguised her softly-rounded femininity.

Having dressed, she turned the steaming clothes of the two men where they hung on a rope stretched across the width of the cave, then peered once more from the cave's mouth. Through fringing foliage she saw the two step back from their work, hands on hips, saw them nod and grin in a self-satisfied manner. The raft was ready. As they began to strain and heave, dragging their craft a little higher up the beach, Aminza put Eldin's tiny kettle on the fire and began to boil water.

For all that their exertions would be keeping them warm, the lake was cold and the mist penetrating. They would be ready for a cup of tea and a bite to eat. Then, a night in the warmth of the cave, stretched out before a crackling, popping fire, with shadows walking on the walls . . . Tomorrow would be a new day. Thinking these thoughts Aminza carefully wrapped Eldin's fire-stones in a scrap of dry skin which she placed in his waterproof pouch. She yawned as she watched the pair shambling up the beach, shoulders slumped.

Yes, they looked bone weary, and she could well understand that. It had been a hard day indeed. Now night was falling, and up above the mists the stars would soon be coming out in the clear skies of dreamland. Who could say but that tomorrow night they might be well away from here, sailing under those very stars, guided ever onward by the pointing knob of Thinistor Udd's wand?

With a glad little sigh, Aminza began to lay out fragrant beds of fire-dried ferns . . .

Morning came in an aching of bones and a throbbing of protesting muscles. It came early for Hero, and when the others awakened from their dreams within dreams he was already returning from the misted beach with a catch of three fine fishes. Thus, when they pushed their raft off an hour or so later, their bellies were full and their spirits high.

In no time at all they drew away from the base of the great cliff and emerged from the mists into brilliant sunshine. A huge blue lake now opened before them, which looked so clean, fresh and unspoiled that Hero was prompted to state:

'You know, I wouldn't be at all surprised to discover that we're the first dreamers who ever chanced this way.'

Eldin sorrowfully shook his great head. 'Ah, no, my young friend! Truth is, I've heard of this lake before. A vast blue lake somewhere beyond the Great Bleak Mountains. Yes!'

'And?' Hero prompted.

'Eh?' grunted Eldin. 'Well, this is it.'

'And that's all?'

'Why, what else should there be?' the older dreamer shrugged. But he frowned a little and tugged at his beard. Then he snapped his fingers and grinned. 'Ah, yes! There was something else. It's said that the lake feeds a great swamp somewhere beyond Thalarion.'

'What?' cried Hero. 'But how can that be? Thalarion lies in a different region of dreamland entirely. Oh, no, I can't see that at all.'

'Perhaps I have it wrong,' growled Eldin, and he shrugged again.

Aminza had been quiet for some little time but now she spoke up. 'This is a queer lake, sure enough,' she said, 'but Thinistor's wand is stranger by far. Does it imagine we're fishes, d'you think?'

They could see what she meant. Dangling from a line strung between two upright poles, the wand still pointed north, but its downward-pointing angle was steeper then ever before. Could it be, they wondered, that the second wand lay deep beneath the waters of this vast lake?

'What makes you say the lake is queer?' Hero asked of Aminza.

'Well,' she answered, 'for one thing it's too quiet – you know what I mean?'

Eldin nodded patiently. 'It's quiet, yes, of course it is – but the sun is shining bright enough. Nothing queer about that.'

Aminza shuddered. 'No,' she said, 'that's not what I meant. It's an *unhealthy* quiet. The air is far too still. There's no wind at all. It's like the lull before a storm. And for another thing –'

'Yes?' Hero prompted.

Aminza sighed. 'You stopped paddling some time ago,' she pointed out, 'and yet we're still making a good forward speed.'

'Eh?' said Eldin. 'How can you tell?'

'I dropped a length of twine over the side,' she explained, 'with a twig tied at its end. The twine is now at full stretch and the twig's bobbing along nicely in our wake!'

'A current?' said Hero, the hair starting to rise at the back of his neck. 'But whoever heard of a lake with a current?'

'And look!' cried Eldin, pointing a shaking finger at the steadily darkening water, where wavelets had sprung up from nowhere to collide and froth in a foamy spray.

'And that's not all,' yelled Aminza as a wind suddenly blew up and snatched at the hair and clothing of the three. 'Just look at Thinistor's wand now!'

They looked – and saw the difference at once. The wand no longer pointed north. Now its knob held waveringly to a north-easterly direction, and even as

144

they watched it turned more fully to the east. Not only that but its angle had grown much more steep, so that it pointed downward at some sixty degrees directly into the lake.

Three pairs of eyes followed the pointing knob, and three sets of hackles rose as the dreamers spotted, some hundred yards away, a circular area of lake where the water shone dark blue and threw up a hazy mist of spray.

'*Whirlpool!*' cried Hero as the raft tilted a little in the suddenly rushing water. 'We're caught in a whirlpool!'

'Hang on for dear life!' roared Eldin. 'Here, Aminza, let me tie you down – and hang onto our supplies whatever you do!'

Feverishly they worked as the raft turned about the dark core of the descending chute. They lay flat and spread their bodies across the deck, lashing themselves and their bundles securely to the heaving members of their pliant vessel. And all the time the raft tilted farther onto its side and rushed faster and faster about the central funnel.

Soon, from where they lay flat on its deck as the raft churned wildly round and round, the three could look down the slope of the whirlpool into its very throat; and now the turning circle of the raft was such that they grew dizzy with its whirling. Thinistor's wand, too, still suspended from its line, was obliged to spin in order to aim its knob constantly into the centre of the maelstrom, pointing out with some demon instinct the shortest route to its closest contemporary, which seemed most certainly to lie at the bottom of the lake.

And again the raft tilted, so that Eldin and Hero gasped aloud and Aminza gave a little scream as the deck became near-vertical. Then – a final jerk and a tilt – and an all-enveloping darkness as the raft slid down, down, down the great and glassy throat of the whirlpool.

The three knew that this was the end – and so were astonished to discover that it was not; for after some time the raft tilted again, regaining something of its former stability, and yet again, until it rushed along horizontally, though still it spun in crazy gyrations upon its own axis.

Now the damp and swirling air was filled with an eerie luminosity, a sort of *ignis fatuus* that danced upon the raft's logs, upon the bodies and faces of its passengers and their bundles . . . and upon the walls and roof of the stalactite-draped tunnel through which they now raced at a fearful speed!

For indeed they had reached the lake's sinkhole – had reached and passed through it into the mighty sump which drained the lake – and now they were bound for some unknown sea of dreamland's nether-caves, wherein the waters of the whirlpool must surely empty. And at last Hero remembered Eldin's words: that the lake fed a great swamp somewhere beyond Thalarion. Perhaps it was so after all; for space in the dreamlands was often paradoxical as time itself, and distances could be more than deceiving.

Sick with the motion of the raft, the three adventurers lay with lolling heads and prayed for death or whatever other future might await them; anything but the continuation of this nauseous ride. They watched the rough ceiling of the tunnel rush by, festooned with stone daggers, often mere inches away from their faces, and they felt doubly ill in the rotten and unnatural glow that lit their way as they rocketed along, seemingly through one of Hell's deepest bowels.

Then –

A light showed ahead. The clear light of day as opposed to the already fading, blue luminescence of the tunnel; and as the dim white glow became a glare so the tunnel widened and the speed of the raft slackened a little. Minutes passed and the disk of light ahead grew larger, then expanded in a final mad burst of speed and was upon them in a moment.

And out into open air they shot, propelled by a veritable spout of water, skipping over scummy depths like a stone spun by some Titan child, each bounce jarring and bruising them until their bodies felt pulped . . . and finally the raft came to rest in tall reeds and lolling bullrushes.

For a long time the world turned round and round and Hero suspected that his brain must be permanently damaged. It must have been shaken loose inside his skull. A quarter of a mile away a tall cliff loomed, spouting water from a resurgence near its base. This was the emergence of that subterranean river which had spat them out like a pebble from a slingshot.

Feeling a little strength returning, Hero loosened the lashings that still held him fast and sat up. He was immediately sick into the reeds and rushes. Eldin, too, was now conscious, cursing and groaning where he lay fumbling at his fastenings. Hero, when he had recovered from his nausea, went to his assistance, freed him, then turned weakly to Aminza. A great bump on her head was turning blue, but her bosom rose and fell with a steady, reassuring rhythm.

'Well,' Hero groaned and held his head for a moment, 'and this must be your great swamp somewhere in Thalarion's hinterland.'

'So it would seem,' answered the older dreamer, tenderly examining his mass of bruises.

As life slowly flowed back into them the two

questers stared about at the swamp's desolation. Some clear water existed between the raft and the cliff with its great jet of water. As for the rest: it stretched away, an endless morass of dead and shrouded trees, reeds and weeds, nodding bullrushes and gloomy papyrus. Strange orchids grew in the mushy stumps of rotted trees; vines hung everywhere, dipping knobby thin fingers in scummy soupy pools. Full of morbid plant life the lake most certainly was, but of flesh-and-blood creatures there was never a sign.

Then, staring into weed-choked distances and feeling the heat of the noonday sun upon their heads, the dreamers heard Aminza's waking cry – a strange little choking cry – and turned to her.

A green vine had crept up over the lip of the raft and was tightening about the girl's throat!

III
THE TREE

With a cry of horror Hero threw himself down beside Aminza, slashing at the vine with his knife. When he had hacked the thing loose from her he sliced at her fastenings and hauled her to her feet, propping her against one of the raft's upright poles. Then he picked up the severed piece of vine, shuddering at its twisting and twining in his hand. Its underside was lined with tiny green suckers which opened and closed and pulsed in hideous hybrid death-throes.

Eldin snatched the thing from him and gave a cry of loathing as he tossed it away from the raft into the morass . . . and a second cry as the scummy surface instantly erupted in a green writhing of hungry life. The whole swamp was a seething den of carnivorous creepers and tentacled plants.

'What in the name of –?' Eldin choked. 'What lunatic of a mind nightmared this lot?'

Hero wasted no words. He snapped long branches from a dried-up tree standing close to the raft and handed one to his burly companion. 'Get poling,' he snarled. 'Head for the open water there.'

Aminza, still disoriented, hung on grimly to the now wobbly uprights as Hero and Eldin used their branches to propel the raft through the morass. No sooner was their craft moving, however, than a dozen more of the suckered vines came snaking hungrily over the edges of its platform.

Hero threw down his branch on the deck and whipped out his curved blade. Razor sharp, the Kledan sword severed wherever it touched and in another moment the raft broke through into open water.

'No use heading for the cliff,' Hero panted, snatching up his pole. 'We'd be smashed to bits by that great spout of water. Run parallel with the cliff until we find a bank.'

Desperately the men poled through waters which were quite shallow, and as they began to make some headway so Aminza stated: 'At least we're going in the right direction. According to old Thinistor's wand, that is.'

Looking back Hero saw that she was right – that the knob of the suspended wand pointed straight ahead – but he also saw something which was far less gladdening. Following them from the seething mass of tangled vines and bullrushes, winding after them through the scummy water, came a tapering, snake-like member which was thick as his wrist.

'Pole faster!' he cried, but in another moment the great vine had reared up out of the water and lashed itself to Eldin's leg. Mercifully, it also trapped one of the raft's uprights, so that it was unable to pull the older dreamer overboard.

Hero's sword gleamed in the hot sunlight as he once again tossed his pole down and leaped to his friend's aid. His blade and Eldin's chopped into the vine together, severing it in two places, so that two great lengths of it flopped about the deck as the damaged parent limb thrashed the scummy waters to a foam in their wake.

Mouthing curses the weary dreamers kicked the writhing sucker-lined lengths of vine overboard and yet again took up their poles. Behind them the entire jungle of living green throbbed and tossed in a sort of fury, and despite their bruised and battered bodies the men needed no urging to toil frantically and put as much distance as possible between themselves and the enraged denizens of the swamp. But by now they were clear of the morass proper and the water ahead seemed calm and harmless enough . . .

Half an hour later they beached the raft on a grassy bank where the cliffs were split by the bed of a dried-out stream. Here, as soon as they had recovered from their long-sustained ordeal of terror, they might easily scale the cliffs and be on their way again. Eldin made a fire well away from the water's edge and brewed tea while Aminza took dried meat and figs from a pack. For his part, Hero spent some time recovering various bits of rope from the raft and pushing its now sadly defunct members back into the water. Some of them might find a mooring somewhere and take root.

After eating, the three adventurers found themselves unbearably weary . . . but not so tired that they were willing to sleep within sight of the swamp. So they shouldered their packs and made their way up the bed of the dead stream until they reached a place where shrubs grew in abundance on the sides of the gorge and they could easily climb to the top. For all that it was a safe, simple climb, they were just about all in by the time they stood on the summit.

Now they found themselves on a gently undulating plain of short grasses and flowers, bushes and shrubs that stretched away southward into low, distant hills. Finding themselves a wild apple tree for shade, they made down their beds in the warm, semi-tropical afternoon and were all three asleep in the twinkling of an eye.

*   *   *

They awakened together from dreams within dreams, to a sky already turning dark-blue with the stealthy encroachment of evening. They sipped tea and ate an apple each, then shouldered their packs and walked in moon- and starlight across plains which were soft beneath their feet, with a springiness that somehow eased their bumps and bruises. And always the wand pointed the way ahead.

'Just suppose this is Thalarion,' said Hero after a while, 'which I suppose it is. What do you know about it?'

'First off,' Eldin answered, 'I know that this isn't Thalarion.'

'But you said –' Hero began.

'I said that the swamp lies in the hinterlands *beyond* Thalarion,' said Eldin. 'Thalarion isn't a country – it's a city!'

'I have heard of that city,' said Aminza in a quiet voice, holding tightly to Eldin's great arm. 'Its monarch is the eidolon Lathi.'

'And what pray,' asked Hero, 'is an eidolon?'

'An image, an idea, a flight of fancy,' answered Eldin. 'I think.'

'An idea!' Hero snorted, curling his lip in a certain way. 'A flight of fancy? Ruling a city? It sounds nonsensical to me.'

'Ah! But you're young in the ways of dreams, lad,' said Eldin, shaking his head in the moonlight. 'When will you learn that a nonsense is only something you don't understand or haven't experienced? It's your own ignorance. A faceless gaunt is nonsensical – until there's one looking right at you! So is a vine with suckers – until you get one wrapped around your leg!'

'I have heard other things of Thalarion,' said Aminza, even more quietly.

'I'm not sure I want to know of them,' said Hero. 'If your tiny little whisper is anything to go by, I'm sure they'll be unpleasant.'

'Say on, lass,' said Eldin, 'and take no notice of him. Forewarned is forearmed, they say . . . I think.'

'Thalarion is demon-cursed,' she said.

Hero stopped walking, turned and took her by the shoulders. 'Aye, I've heard that said before,' his brow wrinkled. 'Though I can't seem to remember where or when.'

Aminza frowned back at him and the stars shone in her big eyes. 'Also,' she continued, 'It's said the eidolon Lathi rules over a hive of horror!'

Now Eldin took hold of her. He shook her a little, but gently. 'Now, now, now,' he rumbled. 'We don't even know if we're going to Thalarion yet – or even where the city lies. We're following Thinistor's wand, that's all.'

'Let's forget Thalarion, eh?' suggested Hero. 'Look, it's a beautiful night and we've a way to go. We'll see the sun up, breakfast on wood pigeon eggs, sleep till noon, then carry on to journey's end. What say you?'

'I say,' answered Eldin, squinting ahead, '– I say we're heading straight for that tree there. The one with the moon standing above it.'

Ahead, atop a low rise, the topmost branches of a tree showed as a black silhouette against a blue-black sky full of stars. Hero stared, then said: 'There must be something wrong with my eyes. Plainly the tree stands atop the hill, or just beyond it, and yet somehow the perspective is all wrong.'

'It's just an effect of the night,' said Eldin.

'No,' Aminza shook her head. 'I can see what David means. Look, the outline of the hill is sharp, but the silhouette of the tree seems indistinct, distant.

I wonder why?' Thalarion was forgotten now in the light of this new mystery.

In silence the three trudged up the hillside and soon stood upon the summit. 'Well, there's one question answered,' grunted Eldin, and he whistled his amazement.

A mile, perhaps two miles away, the tree stood on a plain that dipped gently down toward a distant sea. Its shape was that of a beautiful brandy glass . . . but it towered at least a third of a mile into the night sky!

'I have heard of just such a tree,' said Eldin wisely as they made their way down the slope of the hill to the plain.

'But of course you have,' Hero yawned mightily. 'Is there anything in all dreamland that you haven't heard of?'

'Don't knock experience, lad,' the older dreamer growled. 'Anyway, I was at a banquet in Ulthar some years before we met. This was toward the end of the Bad Days, if I remember correctly. The feast was in honour of a pair of mighty dreamers, men of the waking world – indeed of many worlds – named Titus Crow and Henri-Laurent de Marigny.'

'Ah, now I have heard of them!' said Hero.

'Good! And now that you're satisfied with the authenticity of my tale, perhaps you'll let me finish it? . . . well, the drink was flowing and everyone was in gay mood, and I might tell you that many of dreamland's greatest men were there. And when all the speech-making was done, then they got this Crow fellow to tell a few tales of his trip to Elysia and what he saw there.'

'Elysia?' said Aminza. 'The home of the Elder Gods?'

'The same,' answered Eldin. 'This Crow is a very

154

special fellow, you see, and he has a special place in Elysia whenever he desires to go there.'

'Hmm,' mused Hero. 'That would offend the vanity of the First Ones a bit, I fancy. A mere man allowed into Elysia!'

'Well, possibly – but as I said, this Crow chap is a rather special fellow. Anyway, he told of a tree, just like this one up ahead, growing in a vast garden in Elysia. Moreover, he said that the tree was sentient! It was intelligent and full of love and beauty. There, what do you think of that?'

But before Eldin's companions could answer, all three adventurers stumbled from green grass underfoot onto a powdery surface of crumbling soil, and in the moonlight they could see that this most peculiar path led straight as the flight of an arrow to the foot of the green giant rearing its massive trunk and branches less than half a mile away across the plain. Moreover, Thinistor's wand continued to point in precisely that direction.

'And you think this tree could be related to that other great tree in Elysia, do you?' asked Hero as they followed the sandy path toward the shadow of the giant.

Eldin shrugged. 'Can't really see how that's possible,' he answered.

'A pity,' said Hero. 'After all we've been through, I could do with a little love and joy and beauty!'

Soon the moon began to disappear behind the great tree's bulk, and then the dreamers trod more warily in starlight and occasional moonbeams; and as they passed into the shadow of the tree, so a hush fell over them and they stopped talking and even breathed more quietly. Now the tree towered overhead and they passed under its outermost branches, making never a sound as their paces grew shorter and slower.

Cool, hanging tendrils touched them as they passed beneath and soft-edged leaves as long as a man softly brushed them. The gloom seemed full of weird energy, an almost electrical excitement, as if they tip-toed across the chest of some sleeping behemoth beyond imagination.

Then Aminza tripped on a root and gave a little cry as she flew into Eldin's arms – and immediately the tree came to life!

'Who goes there?' demanded a throbbing, tremulous voice from nowhere – from everywhere – as leaves lashed and retreated and tendrils groped uncertainly in darkness. 'What treachery is this? Does Lathi send out her Ter-men to steal my tender leaves under cover of night? Speak, I say!'

Wild-eyed the dreamers stared about in leafy gloom, and in another moment strong tendrils had found them and snatched them up like bobbins on threads, passing them higher and higher into the tree's heart.

Suddenly Hero discovered one of his arms to be free and he whipped out his curved sword. Eldin heard the *hiss* of his friend's blade unsheathing and saw its gleam in a stray beam of moonlight. Even as they were rushed aloft he called out:

'Stay your hand, lad, or you'll doom us all. It's a long way down if he drops us! Besides, he won't harm us. At least –'

'– You don't think so!' Hero breathlessly finished it for him.

And a second later all three adventurers were dumped without ceremony into the crotch of a great branch a thousand feet above the ground . . .

IV
THE TREE'S TALE

No sooner did Hero feel the bark of the branch beneath him than he leapt to his feet. 'Hell's teeth!' he yelled, blindly waving his sword. 'I've really had enough this time, Eldin. Sucked in by a whirlpool and sicked up in a swamp – victimized by vampire vines and chased by frenzied foliage – and now tackled by a Titan tree? Damn it to hell, where's it all to end?'

'Right here and now if you don't stop dancing about,' Eldin replied with feeling. 'Have you any idea how high we are?'

'Yes, do sit down, David,' said Aminza crossly. 'He doesn't like you stamping about like that!'

'I don't give a damn what the old duffer likes or doesn't like,' Hero shouted. 'I –'

'I didn't mean Eldin,' she cut him off, and Eldin gave a pained snort in the dark.

'Eh?' Hero asked, suddenly deflated. 'Then who did you mean?' He sat down beside his friends and peered at them in the leafy darkness. Now that his eyes were growing accustomed to the gloom he could see that slender green creepers enwrapped them and huge soft leaves trembled above them like great listening ears.

'If you'll only sit still a minute and put your sword away, he'll talk to you, too,' said Eldin. 'Damned if

157

I'd converse with someone who threatened to cut my tendrils off.'

'You haven't got any bloody tendrils!' cried Hero, but he nevertheless sheathed his sword. No sooner was the blade out of sight than several tendrils fell down from above and settled tentatively on his shoulders. A great leaf unfurled close by and brushed his face. At first the touch of these appendages made him start, at which the leaf and tendrils immediately drew back, but as soon as he settled down they approached once more and at last he was permitted to know the source of that throbbing yet ethereal voice he had heard down on the ground.

'Ah!' said the voice. 'But you are an angry one – and therefore you are not of Lathi's brood, for they are without emotion. No, you are a man of the waking world, as is your companion. You are a pair of wandering dreamers, adventurers in Earth's dreamland; and the girl – she is a *real* girl!'

Hero took in all the voice said but was at first too astounded to answer. For he knew now that he heard the tree's voice *in his mind* – that its messages were sent to him telepathically through the tendrils – which would have been an amazing trick even for a wizard, let alone a tree. And the tree could hear his mind as well as it would hear the spoken word.

'Oh, I'm no wizard, David Hero. I'm the Tree, that's all. But I am a rather special tree.'

And yet again Hero was stumped; for what does one say to a tree? Aminza, on the other hand, was positively voluble and full of questions. 'But who *are* you?' she asked out loud. 'And how did you get here? And what did you mean about the eidolon Lathi's – Ter-men? – coming to steal your leaves?'

'Slowly, my child, slowly,' said the Tree, stroking her face with a great downy leaf. 'It's a wonder I've not altogether forgotten how to talk to people, for my visitors have been few indeed in the hundreds of years since the eidolon Lathi built her city on the southern coast. There once was a time when I'd meet, oh, a dozen wanderers in any given year – aye, even a few from the waking world – but all of that is finished now.' The Tree's branches soughed in a great sigh before he continued. 'A pity, for men are full of wonder. Now –' (and it was as if the Tree gave a sad shrug), 'now all has changed.'

'What has changed?' asked Aminza. 'And what is it that makes you so sad?'

'Ah, no, my child,' answered the Tree. 'My problems are insoluble and therefore can wait. First you must tell me how you are come here and why, and then say how I might help you. For I sense that you have troubles at least as great as mine.'

At the Tree's invitation, in bits and pieces, the three then told their story; and when finally they were done it was as if the Tree applauded.

'Bravo!' he told them. 'Well done! And so you have come this far, and you follow the way pointed out by Thinistor's wand. And so inventive, and so daring! You are wonderful creatures. And the size of you, so tiny – but you forge ahead like giants – as I myself should go if things were as they used to be . . .'

'Come, come,' said Eldin gruffly as the Tree lapsed into a troubled silence. 'We've told you our tale, as you requested, and there doesn't really seem to be a lot you can do to help us. So why not unburden yourself on us? We can listen as well as you, you know. And who knows? There may even be some way in which we can be of assistance.'

'Once we know the problem –' Hero conservatively answered.

And so the Tree set about to tell his tale:

'My forebears,' he began, 'grew on a remote world far away in space and time. And their world was vast and there were many of them. Indeed, they were as a forest! Long-lived, the very oldest of Earth's great trees are as saplings by comparison. There came a time, however, when our world began to die, as all worlds must in the end. The air grew chill and the ground froze with the winter of the world, and spring nevermore came. One by one the race of Great Trees died, and sheets of ice moved inexorably across the whole planet.

'On one small island in what had been the tropics, in an acreage sufficient only to sustain them, stood the three last Trees. In the heart of their topmost branches they tended their life-leaves and mourned the new Trees which might have been but now were doomed. And each day the dying sun's rays were fewer and the cold more penetrating.

'Then, by some miracle of chance, a ship of the Elder Gods found the world of my forebears. The ship bore one of the Chosen Ones of the Elder Gods, who was a man. He was the white wizard Ardatha Ell, also the last of his people, which had been great in primal Pu-Tha. And he had found his way to Elysia alone and unaided, for which reason the Elder Gods adopted him. And now, because he was restless and a wanderer by nature, he ventured out from Elysia among the worlds of space and so came to the world of the Trees.

'There Ardatha Ell found the last Trees, all three of them, and there he remained while they withered and died, for he was much too late to save them. And he comforted them in their dying, which is why the race of Man will always be held dear in the hearts of Great Trees wherever they are found.

'And before they died, the Trees asked a further

boon of Ardatha Ell: that he take their life-leaves with
him on his voyage and plant them in warm and gentle
worlds where there would be men and women to talk
to. He agreed, and when the three Trees shed their
life-leaves and settled down to die, gathered up the
golden life-leaves and bore them to his ship.

'Thus, when Ardatha Ell left that frozen world circling under its cinder sun, he carried with him the
entire future of the race of Great Trees.

'Now eventually, he returned to Elysia, home of the
Elder Gods, and there he planted one of the three
life-leaves in the mountain-girt Gardens of Nymarrah
where it grew into the most fortunate Tree! I cannot
swear to this, however, but such are the rumours I've
heard over the centuries. Of the second Tree I can tell
you nothing, for no word of him has since reached
me; but I assume that indeed Ardatha Ell planted him
also. And of course I myself am the third Tree, whose
life-leaf the white wizard planted here in Earth's
dreamland all those thousands of years ago on his way
back to Elysia.

'Now I nurture my own life-leaf, which you may see
if you desire, against the time of my dying, when I will
release it to drift on the winds of dream to some lovely
land, there to live and grow in splendour. And alas –
the day of my dying may not be too far away . . .' The
Tree paused.

'Come now,' cried Hero, suddenly aghast at the
thought of this magnificent creature's dying. 'Explain
yourself. What can possibly harm you here on this
verdant plain? And why would any one or thing desire
to harm you in the first place?'

'Why indeed?' whispered Aminza. 'For you must
be the very gentlest of beings.'

'Patience, my children,' signed the Tree in a
soughing of branches, 'and let me finish my tale . . .

'When first Ardatha Ell planted me here the plain was warm and green and lovely; even as it is now, with one exception, of which I shall speak presently. My rooting was lengthy, however, and centuries passed before the great network of roots which supports me became established. Even then nothing of me showed above the surface for my life-leaf had long returned to dust. And it was just as well that I remained – so to speak – dormant, for all that long time.

'For in Earth's waking world the Northmen were in their ascendance, and they were fierce dreamers. They brought with them snow and ice and mammoths, and for a time it seemed that I, too, like my long dead parent Tree, must shrivel and die in the cold which the northern dreamers brought with them.

'But at length other dreamers came from warmer lands of the waking world, and gradually the climate of the dreamlands swung full circle. Then I put up my trunk and first leaves and drank of the hot sun and cool rains and drowsed in the heady nights of this, Earth's dreamland. And I was favoured here, so that I grew quickly and began my long, slow walk.'

'Your walk?' gasped Hero incredulously. 'A giant like you, and so firmly rooted?'

'Indeed,' the Tree answered. 'Why, you yourself have followed the road I took!'

'The path of dry and crumbly soil!' rumbled Eldin. 'The dead track we followed from the hills to the north.'

'Correct,' said the Tree in a nodding of leaves. 'That was my road. I have walked – however slowly – in the manner of all Great Trees, for that is how giants such as we survive. So great are we that the nourishment we take from the soil rapidly deplenishes it, which means that we must move on or perish. And once the walk is begun, it may only end in the days of our dying. For ten thousand years and fifty miles I have walked, less than one inch every day, and now my journey is almost at an end.'

'But why?' cried Aminza. 'Are you grown old?'

'No, child, not that,' the Tree chuckled, however sadly. 'I am a mere youth in the number of my years.'

'What then?' growled Eldin. 'Why must your walk end here?'

'Because of Thalarion!' the Tree answered, unable to mask a certain bitterness from the three adventurers. 'But there, they are so many and I am only one; and what is my life compared to so many of theirs? Nor shall I truly die, for all of my memories, the memories of my entire race, are locked in my life-leaf.'

'What of Thalarion?' asked Hero, fascinated with the Tree's tale. 'How may the life of Thalarion's peoples so drastically affect your own?'

'I will explain,' said the Tree, and presently continued:

'I have told you of my walk; its mechanics need not trouble you. But as I move along so I send my roots on ahead – deep in the earth, often for distances of many miles – seeking pastures which are favourable to me. Of course, this is a long and tedious process. Certainly it would seem so to you. Also I have my tendrils, many of which are longer than you could possibly imagine. These I send out over the surface, seeking ways between hills and shallow fords across the rivers which may lie in my path. Already I have forded one such river and passed through one such range of hills.

'To the south, beyond the last hills and standing on the shore, there towers Thalarion, the eidolon Lathi's city. Some years ago, knowing nothing of Lathi or her city, I sent my rootlets there, my long tendrils also.

My rootlets discovered the earth to be dry, dead and honeycombed with strange tunnels, and my tendrils found the city where it sprouts above. Ah, and the denizens of that city, they found my tendrils!

'The Lathi's brood, you see, eats only green things, and my tendrils were green and tender. When my tendrils were cut and I felt the pain, then I drew them back to heal them, but in so doing I alerted the eidolon Lathi to my presence. And from that day to this I have known no peace. For it would seem that of all the flesh of all the green things in Earth's dreamland, Lathi and her people prefer mine.'

'That's monstrous!' Hero burst out, leaping to his feet. 'We'll not permit that. Why, there are green growing things galore on this plain! And you say they cannibalize you?'

'Indeed,' the Tree sighed. 'But please sit down.'

Hero sat, but the muscles jumped in his face and his agitation – that of his companions, too – was an almost tangible force in the forest-gloomy air.

'Daily they come,' the Tree continued, 'in their hundreds they come, and I bow down my branches so that they only take the older leaves which are dying; but I can feel in them the desire, the lust for my younger leaves and tender shoots. And ever that lust grows stronger.'

'When do they come? When?' roared Eldin, unable to contain himself a moment longer. 'Damn it, they've a surprise in store!'

'They come in the morning, after the sunrise, and always they leave before noon. And such is their harvesting that I am no longer strong enough to protest it. They sap my strength, you see, forcing me constantly to grow new buds with which to replace the older, stolen leaves. And if I did not bow down my branches, why, then they would steal whatever they could reach! And I would be devastated . . .'

'And they know you for an intelligent, lovely being, these people?' asked Aminza, horrified. 'Do they speak to you?'

'They know it,' the Tree answered. 'And they speak to me, aye, to give me their orders and tell me to bend to them.'

'Are you telling us that *men* do this thing?' Hero cried in outrage and disbelief.

'Ah!' said the Tree. 'They are men, yes, of a sort. But not real men; not like you. They are Lathi's Ter-men.'

'Not real men,' Aminza mused. 'And earlier you said that I was a real girl. Now what did you mean by that?'

'I meant what I said,' answered the Tree. 'That you are real, while the eidolon Lathi's handmaidens are not.'

'Explain that later, if you will,' said Hero impatiently, 'but first tell us why you do not fight back. After all, you have these massive branches, and the great tough tendrils that bore us aloft. Why, Tree, you're a mighty army!'

'I'm a Tree,' the Tree sadly answered, 'and trees burn!'

'They threatened you with fire!' Aminza gasped.

Suddenly, Eldin, who had been quiet for a while, yawned a great yawn that had him stretching his limbs in all directions at once. 'Damn, I'm tired,' he said by way of an apology. 'It's all the walking and talking, I fancy. You know, you two, if we have a fight on our hands in the morning it's best we get some sleep.'

'No!' protested the Tree at once. 'You must not fight for my sake. And the Ter-men are far too many. As for feeling tired: that is my fault. My leaves breathe air but the air which they give out – it is filled with the dust of dreams. Men may sleep as they never slept before beneath a Great Tree!'

Now, in sympathy with Eldin, Aminza and Hero found themselves stifling yawns. In another moment it was more than they could do to keep their eyes open. 'But this is no good at all,' protested Hero as he stretched himself out across the great branch. 'There's so much to talk about, to be explained.' And he yawned again and blinked eyes that refused to stay open.

Aminza, lying with her head on Eldin's massive chest, mumbled something quite unintelligible and Eldin himself began to snore. His snoring was almost volcanic as his waking voice, but Hero's eyes had closed and he did not hear it.

Out of the darkness a great fur-lined leaf descended, covering all but the heads of the three where they lay in their dreams within dreams; and not one of them heard the Great Tree's sigh before he, too, went to sleep . . .

V

THE EIDOLON'S CITY

Hero awoke with a start and quickly stood up. The sun's rays from the east penetrated the Tree's high branches and sent stray beams glancing through leafy shade. Hero peered down at his companions where they lay and saw that they were rubbing the sleep from their eyes. He stretched and stared about – up and down, left and right – at this vast arboreal world which was the Tree. Something had awakened him, but what?

'I awakened you,' said the Tree's voice in his mind, and Hero saw the slender, sensitive tendrils where they coiled upon his shoulders.

'They are coming. Lathi's Ter-men approach!'

'Then you'd best get us to the ground,' Eldin rumbled, climbing to his feet. 'We can't fight them up here!'

'You can't fight them at all,' answered the Tree. 'I thought that was understood? There will be a hundred of them for each one of you.'

'And are we simply to stand and watch it?' asked Aminza. 'I don't think I could bear that.'

'You are to leave me,' said the Tree, 'and save yourselves. I've known of many wanderers who entered Thalarion, but none who came out again. No, you must go back the way you came, or at least give the city a wide berth before you continue on your quest.'

'Yes, well no sense in arguing,' said Eldin. 'You just put us down, right?'

Without another word being spoken, great creepers fell from on high, wrapped about the adventurers where they stood with their packs, lifted them from the great branch – which they could now see was broad as the height of three tall men – and lowered them dizzily into green wells of air. They were passed creeper to creeper with never a pause, and as they went so the great central stem of the Tree – its trunk – rose up above them, like a wall of brown bark. More than a hundred feet through its center, that huge trunk, and at last they stood beside it on firm ground.

'Farewell,' said the Tree, 'and go quickly. Live long lives and be happy. One day you may meet my life-leaf, grown into a Great Tree in his own right, and then we shall talk again.'

'Who said we were leaving?' Eldin growled. He faced Hero and the two grinned their wolfish grins. They shrugged their packs down onto the ground; and then . . . Swords whispered from sheaths and adrenalin flowed in the veins of the dreamers like fiery quicksilver.

Breathlessly, Aminza said: 'David, give me your long knife.'

'No one invited you, girl,' said Hero. 'Tree, take her up again at once!'

'You are very brave and very foolish,' answered the Tree as he snatched Aminza off her feet. 'But you are right about the girl. Yours is not the way she should go.'

'But I want to! I want to!' cried Aminza furiously as the Tree's tendrils quickly drew her up into the forest of branches above.

'Now then,' Eldin rumbled when she was out of sight and sound, 'where are these Ter-men?'

'Remember,' said Hero, 'we have to try reasoning with them first. Especially if they're as many as the Tree says.' He looked up into a vast leafy garden. 'Tree, where are they?'

'On the other side of my trunk,' the Tree's fading voice answered as his tendrils withdrew. 'I put you down on this side so that you could make your escape unseen.'

The dreamers stared at one another and Hero shrugged. He slipped Thinistor's wand out from inside his jacket. 'She still points to the south,' he grunted.

Eldin the Wanderer nodded. 'If we hadn't met the Tree, we'd be heading for Thalarion anyway. Right, let's have a look at the eidolon's Ter-men, shall we?'

They ran swiftly, like large cats, round the bole of the Tree – and pulled up in shock and astonishment on the other side. Whatever else they were, Lathi's people were not the scurvy-looking bunch of degenerates Hero and Eldin had expected. On the contrary.

'So these are Lathi's Ter-men, eh?' said Eldin, mouth agape and sword lowered.

'Some of 'em are, aye,' Hero answered, big-eyed. 'As for the others: I'd guess they are her handmaidens. And handy-looking maidens they certainly appear to be!' And he gave a long, low whistle. For Lathi's Ter-men were tall, handsome and bronzed, with a light yellowish tinge like sick gold. And her handmaidens more than deserved Hero's whistle.

The Ter-men, clad only in papery loincloths, saw Hero and Eldin where they stood. They saw them – and took no notice whatever! 'To hell with *that!*' Eldin snarled through clenched teeth. 'I don't care how many they are, I'll not be ignored.'

'We're not being ignored, old lad,' said Hero. 'Not at all. Look here, will you?' More than a dozen of the handmaidens were flocking forward, dusky-yellow and lovely, all smiles and big brown eyes and bobbing bosoms. They, too, were clad only in loincloths. Six or seven went straight to Hero and approached him not at all shyly. They took his hands and turned him round, openly admiring him and touching him, and one of them adroitly removed his sword and dropped it to the grass.

'I'm not at all sure what Aminza would say about this,' grunted Eldin as he was given the same treatment.

Now, while the Ter-men stood back, blank-faced and with their arms crossed on their deep chests, the luscious handmaidens laughed and danced and played with the two dreamers, leading them a merry chase round and about and tumbling them in the grass. Soon, when they were well away from the Tree's great trunk, Eldin made a strange discovery.

'David,' he called to his friend. 'I'm beginning to understand what the Tree meant when he said the handmaidens weren't real girls.'

'Eh?' said Hero, flat on his back where five of the laughing nymphs held him pinned to the ground. 'They look real enough to me,' he answered, his delighted eyes not knowing which bobbing breast to inspect first.

'P'raps,' said Eldin, a strange note in his gruff voice, 'and right handsome, too – but *real* breasts have nipples, my lad!'

Hero quit his playful struggling and gazed at the naked bosom of the girl who straddled his chest. A moment longer he stared, then gasped: 'Painted on!'

He managed to free an arm and snatched at the girl's loincloth, which tore like paper in his hand.

Now she was completely naked. Hero's gasp became a *hiss* of horror as he looked at her, stared at her where she sat his chest. And then he began to buck his body and thrash his limbs, desperately fighting to be free.

'Eldin!' he managed to choke out his friend's name. 'Nipples aren't all they're missing.'

'I know it,' the older dreamer groaned, fighting his own furious fight. 'The rest of the gear's absent, too!'

Now the handmaidens, showing their true, not inconsiderable strength, held the dreamers firmly down. Those of them not engaged in this began to loosen and tear their clothes from them. The Ter-men, previously passive, now gathered round in a triple-ranked circle two hundred strong. Those on the inside had produced sharp, curved knives like scythes.

The smiles had disappeared now from the faces of the handmaidens and there was something hellish about their gaze as they stripped the dreamers. The Ter-men came closer, lifting up their scythes –

– And as Hero's shirt was ripped from him, so Thinistor's wand fell out upon the grass.

At sight of the wand the half-women sprang up wailing from the dreamers and fled through the ranks of crowding Ter-men. The Ter-men, too, had seen the wand and frowns furrowed their brows as their blank eyes stared. One of them stepped forward, gingerly picked up the wand, retired holding it at arm's length. He immediately set off southward at a trot.

Now the handmaidens came forward again. Unsmiling and yellow, they were suddenly hideous to the eyes of their victims. They motioned to Hero and Eldin that they should stand. Naked and unarmed, the dreamers obeyed, and under the watchful eyes of the thronging Ter-men the handmaidens began to bind them.

This, too, was a shuddersome thing, for the hand-maidens used no ropes but bound the adventurers with threads of sticky, fibrous fluid which they exuded from tiny pulsating orifices in their fingertips! Trembling like trapped flies the captives stood, and in a very short time they were firmly cocooned in shrouding threads as strong and cutting as spun silk.

When their enmeshment was complete, without ceremony the dreamers were bundled over onto their sides and rolled to the outermost area of the Tree's shade. Left with four Ter-men to guard them, they lay in the grass and glumly watched the monstrous harvesting; and as Lathi's half-people worked at the cutting and gathering of the Tree's great leaves, so the two talked:

'Of course,' said Eldin, grinding his teeth, his voice choked with fury and frustration, 'I might have known it. Have you ever been able to keep your hands off a pretty girl? – or ghoul, as the case may be.'

'Me?' cried Hero in amazed outrage. 'Myself? I? And who was it discovered that their breasts were pointless? And *how* did he make that discovery, I ask myself?'

'Powers of observation,' Eldin answered indignantly. 'And if you ever mention that to Aminza, I'll –'

'Shh!' shushed Hero, and whispered: 'Great oaf – they don't know of Aminza!'

'Ah!' Eldin grunted, lowing his voice. 'An error. But look, I don't think these fellows are greatly interested in anything – certainly not in our conversation. They remind me of something – but I don't quite know what it is. They're like machines, or insects, maybe, which have always looked like machines to me.'

'I know what you mean,' Hero answered, 'and you're right. They do seem like parts of some strange machine, each with his own bit to do, his own function to perform. Or a great carnivorous flower, perhaps. The handmaidens: they're the bright, inner colours that attract the insects. The Ter-men: they're the cruel jaws that snap shut . . . What do you think?'

'No,' Eldin disagreed, 'more like insects, I'd say.' He frowned, strained, and managed to turn his head an inch or two to peer at Hero where he lay. 'Ter-men!' he snorted. 'Ter-*mites* if you ask me!'

'Termites?' It was Hero's turn to frown. 'Damn me, you could be right! Human – or half-human – termites. And their queen, we're told, rules a hive of horror! But what of the handmaidens? Undeveloped queens, d'you think?'

'Dunno,' Eldin replied. 'I suppose in a real termite's nest they'd be killed off. But we can't liken Lathi's people too much to their insect counterparts. I mean, they're a totally different race. Also, this is Earth's dreamland, and you can't go by natural laws and rules here. Still, I think we're on pretty much the right track.'

'Yes, I agree,' said the younger dreamer. 'I mean, look at the way they're segregated. There are the gatherers, plucking off the Tree's leaves where he's bowed down his branches; and the handmaidens, who do their own damned deceptive thing; and the guards or soldiers, who seem to just stand around with their arms crossed. As for the last: I imagine they'd be a pretty fierce lot if it ever came to a fight.'

'Hmm,' mused Eldin. 'Drones, workers, queens and warriors, eh? A damned funny lot whichever way you look at 'em.'

'Here,' said Hero as a thought struck him. 'We know about the so-called handmaidens, but what about their blokes? I wonder what they've got up their kilts – if anything?'

Eldin shuddered in his cocoon. 'Nothing,' he

answered. 'I've already looked. It's a nasty sight, old son, I can tell you!'

'But how in hell do they –'

'They don't. Not these lads, anyway. If I knew more about termites I could probably supply the answers. Presumably Lathi has certain bulls who come equipped, so to speak.'

'With a bit of luck,' said Hero, 'we might even live long enough to find out. Actually, we might be better off than we think. I mean, didn't the Tree tell us that Lathi's people were vegetarians?'

'I've a friend in Ulthar who's a vegetarian,' Eldin answered. 'He's also the finest butcher in the city . . .'

With that the two lapsed into an uneasy silence and watched the Ter-men at their work. While this was going on a pair of tendrils snaked down from the Tree's outermost branches and reached for the dreamers where they lay. The Ter-men who guarded them saw the tendrils, however, and threatened with their scythes. Reluctantly, the sensitive green creepers drew back.

The rest of the morning passed quickly and now the sun stood on high. The Ter-men brought up many teams of beasts like tiny Shetland ponies and loaded deep piles of huge leaves onto their travois. Hero and Eldin too were bundled onto one such platform and soon the column of Ter-men, maids and beasts was heading south. In a little less than an hour the Tree was left behind and the column wound through a pass in the last range of low domed hills, emerging on the southern side where the dreamers found themselves within sight and sound of the sea.

There, between hills and shore, where the slope gentled down over earth which was grey, leprous and dead, stood Thalarion. At first, from afar, the few glimpses the dreamers had of the city were blurred

and indistinct with the jolting of their travois; but as
the column neared the city so its structure began to
stand out more clearly. And now they could see how
Thalarion's legend had grown; at least the legends of
its architecture and design.

Certainly from afar – from passing ships, perhaps
– the shunned city would seem a place of towering
spires and awesomely carved turrets; but in fact its
spires were thin and unevenly built, and they only
seemed of a great height by virtue of their slender
contruction. Close up they looked pitted and crumbly
and not at all safe. The lower areas of the city were
grey, sprawling, humped and oddly hybrid; so that
the whole gave the impression of having been designed
by men but built by –

'Termites!' said Eldin, and Hero managed to nod
his agreement.

'Well,' the older dreamer continued, 'that may
answer one question, but it most certainly leads to
another.'

'Oh?' said Hero.

Eldin nodded in his turn. 'What do they want with
us?'

Hero fought against his bonds for a moment, uselessly, then did his best to shrug. 'We'll soon find out,
old lad,' he said. 'Too damned soon, I fancy.'

In a little while the column passed under a domed
arch into Thalarion's musty maze of covered streets
and passageways. The pony-like beasts with their
loads of leaves were led away separately and the handmaidens disappeared along strangely sculpted tunnels
toward unknown destinations. As for the dreamers:
they were taken into the very heart of the hive, and as
they went Hero commented on the city's inner illumi-
nation, a pale blue light which flickered from the
domed, papery-looking ceilings.

'See,' he said. 'There are no real lights – no burning lights, that is. The place is lit by the luminous glow of fungi. It's quite obvious that the Lathi's brood don't much care for fire.'

'They wouldn't,' Eldin grunted. 'Hell, the place is built of paper! Look there –'

One of the walls of the tunnel had developed a crack from floor to ceiling. Specialized Ter-men were at work, exuding a paste from hugely enlarged fingertips, filling the crack with stuff which quickly hardened into a sort of papier-mache. 'That explains their lack of good old asses,' said Eldin. 'No waste in Thalarion.'

'Asses?' Hero looked blank.

'Eh? Didn't I tell you?' Eldin asked. 'They're not only short on marriage-tackle, they've also missed out in waste disposal. As we know it, anyway.'

Hero grimaced. 'You mean to tell me this place is built of –'

'Yes, of a sort,' Eldin cut him off. 'If you want to put it that way. And because this place is made of – er, paper – they can't use fire. They know fire, however, and fearing it mightily they use it as a threat against the Tree.'

'We should burn this damned place down to the ground,' Hero snarled, in answer to which Eldin gave a frustrated grunt.

'Oh, yes – and we'll snap the sparks from our fingers, shall we?'

Before Hero could answer, the older dreamer said: 'Ah, now! We appear to have arrived at our destination, wherever that may be.'

They were dragged from the travois and the beasts were led away. Now Ter-men came up and employed their fingertips in melting away the dreamers' cocoons. They were then given loincloths which they gratefully donned. Four more Ter-men, warriors by their looks, herded them through an archway into a large room which positively glowed with fungous light.

Just inside the archway, the Ter-men paused to hurl Hero and Eldin to the floor. Then they themselves fell to their knees, bowing their heads to the floor in seeming obeisance. From their kneeling positions the dreamers looked about the room, each of them risking a crack on the head from the scythes in the hands of the Ter-men. The place was thronging with handmaidens, and a wide flight of spongy steps led up to a dais against the far wall.

There, atop the dais and flanked by curtained passages, the eidolon Lathi gazed out across her royal chamber. And Lathi was no cold idol. Bathing in a warm glow which had its source at the top of her high throne's backrest, she looked at the dreamers – particularly at Hero – for long moments, then said:

'Welcome, strangers, welcome to Thalarion. Now get up, up – and come to me. We so rarely have visitors . . .'

Her voice, however alien, was full of strange promise and heavy with dreamland's accents. But her face, her body – or at least those parts the dreamers could see of it – was young and indescribably beautiful. As they climbed the wide flight of steps Hero was unable to take his eyes off her. At last he was prompted to whisper:

'Well, old lad, and what do you make of this? I mean, if *those* are painted on, why, I'll stick to twiddling my thumbs in future!'

VI
HERO'S HORROR

At the top of the steps the dreamers halted before Lathi's throne, but while Hero's eyes feasted on the beauty of her face and form, his companion's were busy elsewhere. It was the source of the golden glow in which she bathed which fascinated him. He had known that strange, soft light before – in that secret room in the Keep of the First Ones!

And sure enough, when he stared at its source, he saw that the glow's centre was a Wand of Power where its rod had been thrust like a pin into the high back of Lathi's throne. Now only the knob protruded, and it was this which gave off that rare, steady, golden effulgence.

'Ah!' said Lathi, smiling at the older dreamer, 'you have seen Lathi's Light. It is indeed a wondrous light, is it not? Giving no warmth at all, still it burns like molten gold. Yes, and you offer Lathi as a gift this second rod of magic, which burns not.' She produced Thinistor's wand and waved it in her tiny hand. 'Doubtless it has its use, but I have not discovered it. Perhaps,' she turned her eyes upon Hero, 'you would care to describe its powers to Lathi, and tell her how it came into your possession?'

Before Hero could answer, Eldin growled, 'He would not! And the wand was taken from us, not freely given. Now give it back –' He reached out to snatch the wand from her hand, but before his great fingers could touch it the flat of a scythe struck his skull a resounding *thwack* from behind. Eldin immediately crumpled and Hero turned in a crouch, his hand instinctively reaching for a sword which no longer was there.

'Cowardly dogs!' he snarled at the two Ter-men, who lifted up their scythes threateningly.

'Hold!' Lathi cried, and they froze. Her face, still regal and beautiful, no longer smiled. 'Take that roaring bull away,' she ordered, 'and pen him where he will do no mischief. As for you,' she gazed at Hero and gradually her smile returned, 'you may stay here with me, for now. But understand, neither my Ter-men nor my handmaidens will waver for a single instant if I am threatened. I am their Queen.'

Hero stood still but raged inwardly as Eldin's unconscious form was lifted up and borne down the steps, across the room and out through the arched, sculpted entrance. 'Now then,' said Lathi in her sweet, alien dialect, 'tell me about yourself. Who you are, what you are, and how you came here. I have been told that you are a complete man . . .' Her eyes settled briefly – somewhat eagerly, Hero thought – on his loincloth, then returned to his face.

'I was born intact, yes,' growled Hero. 'Certainly I've got more going for me than your poor lads.' He looked down upon the handmaidens where they stood in groups or reclined upon the floor and frowned. 'Though what good that would do me here is hard to say!'

Lathi saw his meaning and laughed throatily, and so infectious was her laugh that despite himself Hero found his face twitching into a grin. He stared openly at her body. She was naked from the waist up, but

from there on down her form was hidden in volumi-
nous frilly folds of soft paper which were spread out
over the whole surface of her wide throne. Not even
her feet were visible. Hero could not help but wonder
if the rest of her figure matched up to her naked half.

'But you must not think,' she told him in another
moment, bringing his thoughts back to the present,
'that all of my Ter-men are impotent. Indeed not!'
She clapped tiny, delicate hands and the fine paper
curtain to the left of her throne was drawn back. Four
huge, naked Ter-men stepped into view, paraded
before the throne, bowed low to Lathi and hastily
returned whence they had come. The curtain swished
shut behind them.

At the sight of the four – who had been built like
statues of real heroes, and more so in certain
areas – Hero's eyes had widened; but he had noted a
furtive, frightened light in their eyes, though certainly
they had not been frightened of him. Now that they
were gone he forced a couldn't-care-less expression
onto his face and waited.

'You are not impressed?' said Lathi presently.

Hero remembered one of Eldin's favourite sayings.
'I have a friend in Ulthar with very large ears,' he
answered. 'Unfortunately, he's deaf!'

Lathi's smile grew warm as the heart of a sun. 'Ah!
You are wise, and among my Ter-men wisdom is so
rare as to be extinct. Come, sit beside me,' and she
patted the frill-covered seat of her great throne.

Deciding to play along with her for the moment,
Hero sat. She offered him a hand and he took it, and
in no time at all his natural instincts had him stroking
her warm, elegant fingers. Lathi sighed and for a
moment her eyes became half-closed; but then she
petulantly started up. 'And still you have not told me
of yourself!'

'My name is Hero,' he answered. 'David Hero.' He deepened his voice to what he hoped was a seductive purr. 'I'm a man of the waking world – an adventurer in Earth's dreamland – a swordsmaster, keep-climber and wizard-slayer.'

'All of these things!' Her eyes opened appreciatively, perhaps a little mockingly, Hero thought. He remembered something Eldin had told the Keeper – how long ago? – and added: 'And I'm a half-decent singer, too.'

'A singer of songs?' cried Lathi delightedly, and a murmur of anticipation went up from her handmaidens where they now gathered at the foot of the dais. Slowly and deliberately she rubbed her naked shoulder against Hero's where he sat beside her, her great eyes eating him as she gazed into his own. 'And will you sing for me, David Hero? And shall we then discuss other ways in which you might serve Lathi of Thalarion?'

Now while Eldin might definitely argue the fact, Hero was no fool, though occasionally he felt like one. He felt like one now, but at the same time he saw at least a means of prolonging his sudden 'friendship' with the queen of this hive, and thus maintaining his freedom.

His mind had been working overtime since entering the royal chamber, and many small pieces of the puzzle were beginning to fall into place. This was to Hero's liking, for he firmly believed that to find a solution one must first be aware of the problem in its entirety. The longer he remained a free man, the greater his chance of solving the problem, escaping and rescuing Eldin.

'You wish me to sing?' he said, playing for time.

'Indeed,' Lathi answered, 'for the songs of dreamers are so sad and strange, and we so rarely hear them.'

Again he looked round the room, at the Ter-men

where they stood among reclining handmaidens, their arms folded but their strange eyes never leaving him for a moment. 'Ah! But I'm jealous about who hears my songs,' he said on sudden inspiration. 'I don't sing them for men, and I certainly won't sing them for half-men!'

For a moment he thought he'd gone too far. Lathi's eyes clouded for a second or so and her handmaidens uttered 'oohs' and 'aahs' of disappointment. Then Lathi spoke:

'If I send my Ter-men away,' she said, 'and if you should be so foolish as to do anything – untoward? – the handmaidens would very quickly bind you. And then I would have them fill you up with their threads until your stomach, throat and mouth were stuffed with them! That would be a very unpleasant death, David Hero.'

He gulped and agreed, 'Indeed it would!'

'Then we understand one another. Good!' and she clapped her hands.

The Ter-men immediately left the room, going out through the sculpted arch of the great door. And now Hero was alone with Lathi and her – females?

Slowly he began to sing, a lullaby learned in Nir from the matron of a house where once he lodged for two nights. That mother had cared for seven children, singing each and every one of them to sleep in their turn every night. Thus Hero had heard the song fourteen times; aye, and now he remembered how it had put him to sleep, too!

As he sang, so he turned over in his mind the things he had noticed, things which were odd even for a race of people as strange as this one. For instance: the lack of young Ter-men and maids. There were no children. He had not seen a single child in all of this great hive. Were the Ter-men born full-grown? He doubted it.

And then there was Lathi's obvious interest in his manhood, and her hint of a way other than singing in which he might serve her. And what of those prize stallions she had shown him? Were they in reality as useless as geldings?

Still singing, he started as Lathi's head fell softly against his shoulder. It was almost sufficient to bring his song to an abrupt halt, but not quite. Instead, gently turning his head to look at her, he saw that she was fast asleep! Moreover, the handmaidens had all curled up where they lay and were now sleeping. It was unbelievable, more than Hero had dared hope for, and he quickly stifled the *whoop* of victory he felt welling deep in his lungs. No, for victory was still very far away; but certainly his was a tremendous stroke of luck.

Softly crooning, he eased himself off the throne and peered wildly about for a weapon, preferably one of the sharp scythes used by the Ter-men. In that respect, however, he was out of luck, and so turned his attention to the curtains which flanked Lathi's throne. The four great Ter-men he had seen had not been armed, and so this might be a possible escape route. On the run, there were few in Earth's dreamland could outdistance David Hero.

Gradually he let his song fade into silence, then moved soundlessly to the curtain and drew it open a little way. Holding his breath, he looked into the room beyond. At first he could see very little, for the light beyond the curtain was less bright than that of the throne room. Then –

As his eyes grew accustomed to the blue-glowing gloom, so he saw a pair of naked handmaidens slowly and luxuriously rubbing fragrant oil onto a large cylindrical object whose surface gleamed like old leather. The cylinder seemed to protrude from the wall and was all of ten feet long. Big as a barrel at its thickest part, it tapered to a blunt point like a huge chisel. As Hero watched, the thing seemed to shudder in a sort of ecstasy.

Alive? The cylinder was alive! But what in all the dreamlands *was* it?

He could see a little better now and so turned his attention to the activities of the four Ter-men where they crowded together in one corner. Incredibly, they seemed to be gambling – a peculiar sort of relaxation which Hero would not have expected of their species – and he saw the white flash of dice as they rose in air and fell to the hard-packed paper floor.

Quickly, breathlessly the Ter-men scrutinized the dice where they lay and three of them turned their heads to peer at the fourth. For his part he leapt wildly to his feet. The winner, Hero thought, then rapidly changed his mind as the others rose up and grabbed hold of the fourth before he could flee. They held him down while one of the handmaidens left her work on the cylinder-thing to weave a web of silk over his mouth.

Then the three dragged him to the blunt end of the morbidly heaving cylinder and held him while more threads were used to bind his legs together and his arms to his sides. Trussed up like this, he was unable to get his fingers to the threads and melt them – if his type was equipped for that task.

Now the handmaidens began to stroke and massage the cylinder about one third of its length up from the blunt chisel-point. By this time Hero could see quite clearly and he noted once again the undulant, ecstatic motion of the thing as the handmaidens worked on it. His hand began to tremble a little on the curtain as he tried to fathom the meaning of what he was seeing. Something horrible was happening here – or was about to happen – and it seemed to Hero that he should know what it was. Or that he should flee before he found out what it was . . .

Then –

His eyes widened and the hair rose up at the back of his neck as he saw that the cylinder-thing was . . . was opening! At the subtle and practiced urging of the naked handmaidens a long slit had appeared in the leathery surface of the vast sausage-shape. And now it seemed to pulse, that gash, and in a monstrous spasm it opened wider still.

Hero found himself shuddering almost uncontrollably as the three Ter-men picked up their former colleague and held him horizontally in the air. Now what in the name of –?

Somehow Hero stifled his gasp of horror as the Ter-men placed the head of their luckless fellow in the pulsing gash and pushed and shoved until he had fully entered the cylinder and only his feet protruded. Those feet twitched, jerked spastically, twitched again, and finally were still. And suddenly the massive cylinder convulsed, contracted, convulsed again in a loathsome rippling of nameless flesh, which tailed off into a sort of near-inert, exhausted palpitation.

The Ter-men waited a moment longer then tugged at the motionless, protruding feet of their ex-comrade and pulled his body – or what was left of it – clear of the gash which now began to close. The body looked like a time-ravaged mummy, shrivelled and bloodless, a dry skin full of dry bones!

And at last Hero knew it all. In his mind he had measured up the thickness of the wall and had positioned the Queen's throne behind it. He need wonder no longer about Lathi's lower body, so carefully hidden from view while her upper torso was so lusciously displayed. No, for this cylinder-thing, this vast leathery trunk, this *was* the eidolon Lathi's body; and now Hero knew just exactly what she had meant by 'another way' in which he might serve her!

The curtain tore in his hand as he stumbled backward away from the entrance to that awful nuptial chamber; but his low moan of uttermost terror was completely drowned out by Lathi's shriek as she was awakened – by her own passion, perhaps? – to discover his deception.

Seeing him where he stood with the torn curtain in his hand at the top of the steps, she began furiously to clap her hands; and in the next moment there sounded a veritable tumult of shouting and rushing feet from beyond the sculpted archway. As if this were not enough there was something else, something which seemed as much a surprise to the denizens of the hive as it was to Hero: a series of massive subterranean *thumps* that shook the ground as by the tread of some striding giant.

He had little enough time to ponder these tremors, however, but rather worried about more pressing matters. Namely the dozen or so Ter-men who came bursting in through the archway to rush at him up the dais steps!

VII

THE DOOM THAT
CAME TO THALARION

Carried on the shoulders of three Ter-men, Eldin was
not unconscious when he was borne from Lathi's
throne room. He could feel an egg rising on the back
of his head, true, but that was only a temporary thing.
He had come to his senses as soon as he was picked up,
and now he was taking particular note of the route his
bearers took through the paper-built maze to –

– To where?

Was he to be simply disposed of, he wondered, or
would it be a grandiose thing? Whichever, he
wouldn't go quietly. But for the moment it were best
that he lie still and firmly fix in his mind's eye the
tortuous ways that led back to the throne room and
his fellow adventurer, David Hero.

'Hero – *hah!*' thought Eldin, and he was almost
tempted to snort. And the eidolon Lathi, luscious
little plum, making eyes at the young idiot. Why, by
now he was bound to be making eyes right back at
her!

Before Eldin had time to conjure more than two or
three erotic pictures of Hero's present pursuits with
the Queen of the hive, he was tossed rudely into the
black throat of a deep, well-like pit. Some twenty feet

189

down he struck bottom – a mercifully spongy bottom, though sprinkled here and there with hard bits – and lay still while he got his wind back. The place was lighted with the same fungous blue glow of the upper tunnels, which light was supplemented by the rather more rotten luminescence of –

Decaying corpses!

Eldin quickly scrambled away from a pile of stinking cadavers and miscellaneous bones, only to be drawn back a moment later as his curiosity got the better of him. The stench was terrible, and while his fall hadn't harmed him certainly this reeking atmosphere soon would. Gingerly, with his naked foot, he turned over skeletons and kicked aside leering skulls.

The place was a veritable ossuary, a boneyard, and it was plain to see that Thalarion's Ter-men had no favourites when it came to unwanted visitors. No, for the bones and cadavers were of almost every sort and species of dreamland's denizens. There were the skulls and tattered loincloths of the tiny brown people of Kled, and the larger, big-boned corpses of rangy men of Inquanok. There were recently dead, softly-rounded remains of black men of Parg – doubtless escaped slaves from some galley on the Southern Sea – and even horned skulls of the evil, squat, wide-mouthed denizens of Leng's forbidden plateau.

How they had come here and why – that was anybody's guess, but plainly they had all ended up the same way. Yes, and now it seemed that Eldin the Wanderer was to share a like fate. He was not ready to give in so easily, however, and so tried scaling the walls. But the stuff of the walls simply would not take his weight; it came down in handfuls whenever he got a good grip, so that it seemed if he continued he must surely bury himself.

Just then, as he paused to think again, he felt a

tremor in the pulpy, paper foundations of the place. He stood stock still and silent, waiting, and after a moment there came another subterranean shock. A small earthquake, perhaps? A series of them? Or had a couple of Thalarion's fretted spires rotted through and toppled down onto the city? Eldin hoped so, and also that a good many Ter-men had been crushed or smothered, but he doubted it.

He was still pondering the mystery when, a moment later, there echoed from on high the sounds of a struggle and a voice he had thought never to hear again. Shouting her defiance, gasping and crying all at the same time, Aminza was giving someone an awful lot of trouble up there. The sounds came closer, and with one last shriek of defiance Aminza was pitched down into the hole. Eldin, directly beneath her, was able to catch hold of her arms and so cushion her fall a little, but still they were both dashed down to the pulpy floor.

Then, quick as a flash, Aminza had elbowed him in the ribs, was up on her feet and had her back to the wall. Eyes blazing in the blue-glowing gloom, she cried: 'Come on then, whoever or whatever you are. Come and get your eyes scratched out!' And she held up her hands before her, fingers crooked and ready to strike.

'Damn me, girl,' Eldin wheezed, getting his breath back where he sat on a broken skull, 'I'm not sure I want to marry you after all!'

'Eldin?' she gasped. 'Eldin?'

'Aye, it's me all right,' he said, climbing wearily to his feet and staggering as a third tremor set the whole city shaking. 'But what the devil's happening, girl? Are you in some way responsible for these shocks that keep rocking the place?'

'Not me,' she cried, flinging herself into his arms. 'I

don't know what it is – but it feels like the city's about
to fall down about our ears!'

'Well, at least we'll be together if it does,' he
answered. 'Now then, you'd best tell me how you
come to be here.'

Breathlessly she explained how from the heights of
the Tree she had seen the dreamers taken prisoner,
and how then she had slipped away from the Tree and
followed the column of Ter-men to Thalarion. From
the hills she had watched them enter the city, had then
sneaked closer and crept inside. She bore no weapon
with her, no plan of action in her head, but only knew
that she must rescue her friends if that were at all
possible. If not, then she would share their fate. A
body of Ter-men had picked her up almost immediately and had obviously deemed it wisest not to take
her to the eidolon Lathi. The Queen would not toler-
ate another whole female in her hive. Thus she had
been dumped into the pit, there to starve and join the
bones of them who went before.

'Brave but foolish,' Eldin growled, hugging her to
him in the gloom. 'It seems the old Tree was right
about us, eh?'

She nodded her head against his chest in agreement
and a little sob escaped her trembling lips. 'Oh,
Eldin!' she whispered.

'Don't be frightened, girl,' he patted her abstract-
edly. 'Things will turn out all right – I think.'

She looked about at the contents of the pit, staring
hard as her eyes grew accustomed to the shadows,
then once more buried her face in Eldin's chest. 'If
only it wasn't so gloomy,' she sobbed. Then – '*Eldin!*'
she cried, and danced away from him in a sudden fever
of excitement.

'Eh? What?' he cried. 'What's up, lass?'

'Your pouch!' she answered. 'I've brought your

pouch. I'd forgotten about it till now. Here –' and digging a hand into her shirt she came out with Eldin's waterproof pouch.

He took it from her, thumbed its contents through the outer skin and slowly shook his head. 'I know what you're thinking, girl, but forget it. If I struck a light down here, with all these rotten gases swirling about – *whoosh!* – the place would go up like tinder, and us trapped in the middle of it. No, I can think of better ways to die. Here, put the pouch away.'

As she took back the pouch the ground shook yet again, and this time the piled bones and mummies literally erupted in a cloud of decaying debris. Something groped upward from the floor, swayed in the bluish light, fell writhingly against the pair where they crouched beside the wall.

'What the devil –?' Eldin snarled, then relaxed with a great sigh of relief as a voice in his mind said:

'I've found you – at last!'

'The Tree!' cried Aminza, her hand on the shuddering root.

'Part of him, at least,' said Eldin, and to the Tree: 'Was that you shaking the city?'

'Indeed. Did I not tell you that my roots had already discovered Thalarion, finding the soil beneath the city dry and dead? It offers them little or no resistance. I only hope I've strength enough to complete my task – which is to bring demon-cursed Thalarion to the ground!'

'We'll do more than that, old friend,' cried Eldin out loud. 'But first – can you get us out of this pit?'

'Wait,' answered the voice in his head as the root withdrew. A moment later it reappeared, bursting through the wall close to the very top of the pit. Down it snaked to where Eldin and Aminza could grasp it.

'Climb, climb!' cried the Tree's voice in their heads.

'You first, lass,' said Eldin, pushing her from behind. 'Up you go.' To the Tree he said, 'How much damage do you think you can do?'

As Eldin began to climb, the Tree answered. 'I can destroy Thalarion – though that will be the end of me. There are bound to be survivors, and I know what they'll do to me. At least I'll go in a blaze of glory!'

'Very brave and very foolish,' answered Eldin with a savage grin as he climbed out of the pit directly behind Aminza. 'Tree, what prompted you to do this?'

'You and Hero were willing to give up your lives for me, and Aminza was willing to die for you. And so –'

'So you're willing to burn in order to give us a chance, eh? But what if Thalarion has no survivors?'

'How can that be?'

'You just do your bit, old twig,' grinned Eldin, 'and leave the rest to me!'

'What else may I do to help you?' asked the Tree.

'You can try to find Hero and see if he needs a helping hand – or root,' the scarfaced dreamer answered. 'And you'd best be on your way now so that I can get this thing started. How many of you – er, *much* of you – is there under the city anyway?'

'A lot of me,' answered the Tree. 'And for now, farewell.'

The root withdrew, was gone in an instant, and now the two stood alone at the edge of the pit . . . for a second only. For as the tremors began again, stronger now and more insistent, so a pair of Ter-men emerged at a run from the mouth of a nearby passageway. For a moment it looked as if they might go on their way, but then they saw Eldin and Aminza at the edge of the pit. They had scythes and lifted them up as they rushed upon the pair.

Without ceremony Eldin shoved Aminza to one side. He snatched at the first Ter-man's scythe arm, pulled, ducked and lifted all in one flowing motion, drawing his attacker up onto his own brawny back. They were after all not used to fighting, these Ter-men, and Eldin held his victim across his shoulders in a wrestling hold as he spun, knocking his second assailant flying. Then, tossing the dizzy creature from his shoulders into the pit, he turned and kicked the second Ter-man in the throat as he made to get to his feet. With a gurgle that told of a smashed windpipe the Ter-man fell back. Eldin snatched up his fallen scythe, pounced on him and dispatched him with a single stroke.

'Here, lass,' he grunted, turning to Aminza. 'Take this.' She gingerly accepted the crescent blade, twisting her mouth at sight of the thin yellow fluid which served the Ter-men as blood.

'No good going all squeamish now, Aminza,' Eldin told her. 'There's some damned rough work ahead and I've no doubt you'll need to do your bit. Now then, give me back my pouch, will you? I think we'll have a little more light on the scene.'

He tore fragments of paper from a wall, struck sparks from his firestones, tossed the makeshift brand into the pit behind them. With a rush and a roar that hurled both of them flat, a huge column of flame instantly gouted up from the pit and rivers of fire ran rapidly across the high ceiling.

'I told you it would be a hot one,' Eldin yelled, gathering up the girl. 'Come on, let's go!'

With Eldin slightly in the lead, they ran along the passage which led back to the throne room. As they went the glow of the fire behind them lit the way ahead for a short distance, panicking three Ter-men where they already stumbled to the now continuous shuddering of the foundations.

Without pause Eldin snatched the scythe from one of them, cut down the second and knocked aside the third; then grabbed Aminza's hand once more and ran as fast as his legs could carry him. Whenever they came to a junction of passageways, there they would halt for a few seconds while Eldin set fire to the walls; but now at last they approached the throne room proper.

Here, in the maze of passages, corridors and tunnels which surrounded Lathi's chambers, a large number of Ter-men and maids were rushing aimlessly about in a frenzy of panic. Eldin and Aminza, for all that they stood out like sore thumbs, found themselves almost totally ignored – but the scarfaced dreamer was never one to be ignored for very long.

With a whoosh and a roar he set fire to one last junction of burrows, then dragged Aminza after him under the high sculpted archway which he recognised as the entrance to Lathi's throne room. They came to a breathless halt just inside the room and took in the scene at a glance.

The place was awash with a sea of milling Ter-men and maids; and atop the dais steps Hero battled desperately against huge odds, using catlike speed and brute strength to hold the steps against a crush of scythe-wielding Ter-men.

'Hero, catch!' roared Eldin, and sent a scythe whirling through air, straight to the hand of the younger dreamer. And after that confusion turned to chaos.

Within seconds the archway was blazing and Eldin and Aminza were battling their way through Lathi's dazed and disbelieving minions toward Hero. By the time they reached the foot of the dais its steps were already awash in the yellow blood of slain Ter-men. Atop the steps, berserk as any Viking ancestor of the waking world, Hero was drenched with the stuff where he stood astride a pile of Ter-men bodies.

What with the slime on the steps and the now crazed heaving and bucking of the floor, it was hard work on the part of Aminza and Eldin to make it to Hero's side; but at last all three stood together. And up through the floor burst the Tree's roots, writhing and wriggling, adding to the chaos, flinging papery debris everywhere as they tore out the very foundations of Lathi's domain.

Eldin deliberately grasped at a root that broke from the wall close by, and was immediately in communication with the Tree. 'Tree,' he yelled out loud, 'We're finished here. Now how do we get out?'

'My creepers,' the Tree responded at once. 'I have two of them directly above you. Just let me give this place one last shake – there!'

The throne room was wracked by tremendous tremors which had the three clinging together for support, and a moment later a great jagged crack appeared in the floor and ran up the wall. Huge areas of the ceiling began to cave in and daylight at once flooded the place. Down from above snaked a pair of tough green creepers which pounced on Eldin and Aminza and hauled them aloft. In another second the creepers were back, this time to lift Hero out onto the city's sagging, sliding roof. In one hand he now carried two wands, one of which glowed with a golden light. Behind him as he alighted on the treacherous roof, a great gush of flame sent a mushroom of smoke into dreamland's late-afternoon sky.

'Tree,' cried Hero where he hung onto the creepers, 'it's time we all got out of here. I don't quite know how you, Eldin and Aminza managed all this, but I do know we're in for a scorching if we don't get moving!'

'I can still help,' answered the Tree. 'Just hang onto

my creepers, all three of you, and run as hard as you can. You run and I'll pull, and with luck you'll be out of the city before it falls flat.'

They needed no second urging but hung on grimly as the Tree's stout creepers dragged them across Thalarion's shuddering, crumbling roof; and all about them the spindly spires of the city were falling into ruin and sending up clouds of dust and rags of shredded paper. Flames gouted up from a dozen points, raced over the roof, licked at the three where they leaped and stumbled through sinking, settling acres of disintegrating paper.

And at last they were sliding down the outer domes, stumbling over dead, dry soil, running for the hills as behind them, roaring its death-agonies to the darkening sky, Thalarion became a mighty, raging inferno. . . .

PART FIVE

PART FIVE

I
FLIGHT OF THE LIFE-LEAF

'Creepers?' chuckled Eldin when the three stood in the hills and watched the Tree's tendrils rapidly retreat northward, drawn back by their mighty master. 'I reckon he should call them runners!'

'How can you be humorous in a charred loincloth?' Hero asked, then shrugged and decided that perhaps Eldin was right. He turned back to face Thalarion, holding his hands out to the distant blaze. 'Cozy little fire, isn't it?' he said.

'Eldin, you were wonderful!' said Aminza, standing on tip-toe to kiss the older dreamer.

'Um,' Eldin grunted in agreement. 'That'll teach them to fool around with Eldin the Wanderer!'

'Not to mention David Hero,' said Hero, slightly miffed.

'Who mentioned David Hero?' Eldin asked. 'What did you do that was so wonderful?'

'Ho-hum!' yawned Hero, examining his rather grimy nails. Carelessly, with an air of it-doesn't-really-matter, he held out the wands for inspection. 'And who was it risked his neck, in the middle of all that was going on, to take back Thinistor's wand *and* lift Lathi's at the same time? After all, that's what we came for – among other things.'

'Personally,' said Aminza, 'I think the Tree deserves more thanks than all three of us put together.' And the dreamers could find no fault with her statement.

So they stood together and watched Thalarion burn, and soon the city was reduced to a fine white ash which the night winds would quickly disperse. The eidolon Lathi's city was no more; the menace of the Ter-men and maids and their monstrous Queen was removed forever from the land of Earth's dreams.

'Why "eidolon?" ' Aminza thought to ask as they began to make their weary way back to the Tree under dreamland's star-strewn skies.

Eldin frowned and shook his head.

Hero said: 'An eidolon is an image or a representation; not the real thing. Well, neither was Lathi the real thing.' And remembering what he had seen in that hideous bridal-chamber behind the throne room, he shuddered and fell silent.

In the morning they found a stream and bathed, washing away all of their accumulated aches and pains. Afterward they got their things together and Aminza did a little repair work on the men's clothing. Through the early afternoon they laughed, joked and talked with the Tree. He would soon begin to 'walk' again, to turn and head east now that the threat was past. His strength would rapidly return and he would live to a ripe old age.

As the day wore on the adventurers played hide and seek amongst the Tree's leaves and great branches, and later they made a fine meal of fish caught in the stream; but in the late afternoon their massive host began to sense their restlessness, and it was then that he sprang his big surprise. He broached the subject as they lay side by side on their backs, with their hands under their heads, across one of his mightiest branches.

Hero sat up at once. 'What was that, Tree? Did I hear you right?'

'Certainly. Before I attacked Thalarion, I prepared the life-leaf. I knew that if I failed to rescue you – even if I succeeded – Lathi would destroy me. I *believed* I would be destroyed, burned down. Therefore, long before his time, I prepared the life-leaf. Once I had fed him the special juices he required to begin his separate life, then there was no stopping the process. Before morning, in only a few short hours, the life-leaf will detach himself and fly free. He will be a complete being in his own right, the life-force from which a new tree shall grow.'

'A clone,' rumbled Eldin.

'Eh? What's a clone?' asked Hero.

Eldin frowned and after a moment said: 'Dunno, but I once knew – I think.'

Hero and Aminza snorted simultaneously and gave their attention back to the tree. Aminza asked, 'And are you seriously suggesting that your life-leaf should carry us on the next leg of our journey?'

'Why not? He is the largest and loveliest leaf I shall ever produce, and unique in his ability to fly. Normally he would seek out his own place, find a land of warm suns, soft rains and fertile soil, but this time you will do it for him. Somewhere, between here and your destination, there must be such a place. There shall the life-leaf take root and grow into a Great Tree.'

'And we can, er, ride him in safety?' questioned Eldin a trifle uncertainly.

'Assuredly. I should perhaps state, however, that life-leaves are full of the natural joys of youth. The journey may well be a little – exhilarating?'

'The more I hear of this,' said Hero enthusiastically, 'the more I like the idea. To ride a life-leaf through the night-skies of dreamland! Why, it's the chance of a lifetime, something no one ever did before –'

'Or ever will again,' said the Tree.

'Exhilarating,' Eldin repeated the word thoughtfully, a little worriedly. 'He's not likely to go looping the loop, is he?'

'Nothing like that,' answered the Tree with a mental chuckle. 'Not with you three aboard.'

'And he'll follow the route we wish him to take?' asked Aminza.

'Of course. That shall be my last instruction to him.'

'Amazing!' observed Eldin. 'Godparents to a tree!'

'To a Great Tree,' the Tree reminded.

'Eh? Oh! Of course, yes,' mumbled the older dreamer apologetically.

'Tree,' said Hero, 'some time ago you offered to show us this life-leaf of yours. Now I'd like to take advantage of your offer.'

'Me too,' said Aminza.

'And me,' added Eldin.

'It grows late,' answered the Tree, 'and soon you'll feel the effects of my sleep pollens.'

'There's time enough,' said Hero, 'and light enough, too!' And he produced Lathi's wand from inside his shirt. The golden glow of the wand was like the light of some mighty firefly guiding them through the gloom as the Tree immediately swept them aloft to that secret heart-place where grew the life-leaf.

And they were properly hushed when the Tree gently deposited them in that network of protective branches in his uppermost regions, where the life-leaf lay unfurled, huge and soft-edged, his pockets filling with buoyant gases from the parent Tree's great trunk, his tracery of veins a-throb with those special juices which had awakened him. Big as a large carpet, the life-leaf – big and beautiful and alive! – a pulse of joy which drew its strength, its seeds of knowledge, its ancient ancestral heritage from the Great Tree, whose pride was a tangible thing in the night.

Silently the three stared, for long and long, and the glow of Lathi's wand lent the scene a properly magical air. Finally, almost as one person, the three spoke to the Tree. Not wishing to destroy the moment, they spoke in whispers, even Eldin.

'Tree,' the older dreamer said, 'it's time for bed.'

'Yes,' Aminza agreed. 'A little sleep won't go amiss.'

'Especially,' added Hero, pleased that he was to have the last word, 'since we're to go a-riding tomorrow!'

Two hours before dawn the Tree awakened them. It was time. He lifted the three and their packs back to that secret place in his highest branches, and there invited them to step aboard the life-leaf. Gingerly at first, then putting their faith in their gigantic host, one at a time they stepped onto the wide, ribbed platform and settled down in the carpet of long, soft hairs which covered it. The leaf's surface gave to their weight with a gentle resilience, its gas-sacks moulding to their shapes and its furred edges curling up a little to form a shallow boat shape.

Hero sat in the 'prow,' Thinistor's wand in hand, holding it lightly and allowing its knob to point . . . westward! Westward, along the coast of the Southern Sea. The faces of the three glowed golden in the light of Lathi's wand, which Aminza held in her lap like some cold, wonderful torch. They were tense now and a little afraid. Each looked to be on the verge of speaking, but no one said anything. Then –

'It's time!' said the Tree.

There came a great soughing of leaves as he lowered his closest branches downward from his trunk to form a sort of ramp, and the adventurers held their breath as a soft tearing sound reached them from the spot where the life-leaf grew from its massive parent body. The sound came again and the life-leaf gave a shudder and tilted slowly downward.

'Ah!' said the Tree. 'Farewell, my friends, farewell!'

The three would later argue whether or not they actually answered him, but not one of them would know for sure. For now they were in motion, feeling the flow of air against their faces as the life-leaf launched himself down a ramp of branches, hearing the swish of soft leaves giving way beneath them to ease the life-leaf's passage. More steeply yet the living carpet tilted and faster its forward, downward rush until, with the very gentlest of bumps –

They were airborne!

And no sooner were they in the air than the life-leaf moved beneath them, shifting and balancing its mass to form an amazingly efficient airfoil. A light wind blew off the sea to greet the oncoming dawn, and the life-leaf sought out its currents and rode them, rode high, until soon the hills, valleys and rivers were left far, far below.

Round and round in a wide rising spiral flew the life-leaf; and his passengers sat, hair streaming, flesh tingling, and gazed down wide-eyed on all the vastly improbable lands of Earth's dreams. Far out over the Southern Sea they spotted the lonely lights of fishing boats and other craft, and away to the east the first rays of the sun were dusting the edge of dreamland with a glow to challenge that of Lathi's wand. Somewhere in the dark, distant curve of the west a city's lights showed momentarily, and in the north the writhing wraiths of aurora borealis performed their ghostly dances.

But by now they had reached those uppermost limits of atmosphere beyond which the life-leaf dare not ascend, for to do so would be to penetrate realms inhabited by the flopping, shapeless and namelessly monstrous larvae of the Other Gods. Here the flight of the life-leaf levelled out and gradually his 'prow' came round to point westward. Then, following the way pointed out by Thinistor's wand, the life-leaf began the long, gentle downward glide which would take the three adventurers to their destination.

Now, because of their altitude, the sun seemed like a blade of blinding light on the horizon far behind them; and as they drifted lower so its dawning rays turned dreamland's rivers and streams to ribbons of silver. Their speed was enormous, and towns, cities and mountain ranges passed beneath almost as quickly as they could be counted. As yet neither the light nor their orientation was such that the adventurers could name for a certainty the territories over which they passed, though certainly there was something very familiar about many of the bays and ports of the Southern Sea.

It was only when they sailed lower still and the mountains reached up toward them that they began to pick out specific places remembered of earlier wanderings. Then in the dawny distance the men of the waking world spied that winding, flashing snake of water which could only be the Tross, and they saw near its mouth the mist-wreathed city of Theelys.

Why, this was where it had all started for them! Right here in Theelys . . .

Down, down floated the life-leaf, its buoyancy

gases streaming out from pockets which emptied themselves, and as if to match or guide the leaf's descent so the knob of the wand in Hero's hand dipped lower and lower. Twice they circled high over the turrets of a castle on Theelys' outskirts, then tilted steeply toward the great gardens within the castle's low outer walls.

The adventurers held on grimly as the life-leaf skimmed trees and tall shrubs, gritted their teeth as it stalled and slipped sideways, and finally sighed in unison as it gentled to the ground and came at last to rest. As they climbed shakily from the settled leaf, slender coiled tendrils like long white worms fell from its stem, burrowed deep into the soil and immediately took root.

'Not the sunniest place in Earth's dreamland,' said Hero, peering closely at the leaf where it now began to wilt upon the grass. 'Still, I suppose he knows what he's doing.'

'I shouldn't worry too much about him, my lad,' said Eldin, the hint of a warning in his deep growl. 'Not just yet, at least. I think we've one or two problems of our own. Look where your wand's pointing –'

Hero looked – and his hand instinctively flew to the hilt of his sword.

For the knob of Thinistor's wand pointed directly at the massive gates of the looming castle, and atop the high inner wall stood a figure in rune-inscribed gown and conical cap, his eyes fixed firmly upon his visitors and the shadow of a strange smile upon his wizard's lips. . . .

II
THE TALE OF NYRASS
OF THEELYS

The wizard beckoned with a rune-clad arm and called out: 'Welcome to the castle of Nyrass of Theelys. I welcome all three of you; and what a singular honour, to be borne here on the life-leaf of a Great Tree! Now enter, enter and fear not. No harm will come to you in the house of Nyrass the Mage – none of my doing, at any rate.'

The voice was thin and reedy with age, but the welcome it extended seemed earnest enough. Cautiously the three approached the castle's moat, crossed it over on a drawbridge of oak, passed under the stone arch of a massively thick wall and so into the cobbled courtyard. Nyrass came slowly down a flight of stone steps from the wall to where they waited for him. His hair and moustache were white as driven snow, as was his waist-long beard.

Now, in the dawn light, they could see that he was very old, and such was the weary smile on his wrinkled but friendly face that their apprehension quickly went out of them. 'Mighty adventurers indeed!' he said, his rheumy eyes upon the wands which Hero and Aminza still carried. 'Since you have that wand –' he pointed an agued finger at Hero's rod, 'it may be supposed

that my cousin Thinistor is no more.' He turned to
Aminza. 'And while you have that wand –' again he
pointed, 'the same must be believed of Lathi!'

'You're right, old man,' growled Eldin. 'Both
Thinistor Udd and the eidolon Lathi are dead. And
you'd have us believe that such news pleases you,
would you?'

'Pleases me?' the wizard answered at once. 'No, it
saddens me, for it means that a little more of magic
and mystery has gone out of Earth's dreamland. Oh,
I'll agree it was probably necessary, but still . . . Both
dead, you say, and by your hands?' He peered at each
of the three in turn. 'My, my! They'll sing songs of
this one day in Celephais and Ulthar.'

'Wizard,' Hero now spoke up, 'we've come a long
way and faced many terrors to get here. We're
questers, and since you've already seen and recognised these wands we've won, well, I'm sure you'll
know that we've come to you for the third.'

'Oh, I know that well enough,' Nyrass answered.
'But I'm sorry, for I can't help you.'

'What?' scowled Eldin. 'But the wand's here. We
know it is!'

Nyrass nodded. 'Indeed it is – but still I say to you
that you can't have it.'

'Be warned, old man,' said Aminza, nimbly stepping between her suddenly tense companions and the
wizard. 'These are desperate fellows when their
blood's up. If you have the wand, you'd do well to
hand it over.'

'I have it,' he answered, taking her hand and
patting it, 'and I don't have it. You'll understand
presently, my dear. But come along, let's not stand
out here all day. We'll breakfast together and then
you can tell me your story. After that, if you wish, I'll
tell you mine – and then you'll know why I can't give

you the third wand. Well, are you coming?'

Hero and Eldin looked at one another for a moment or two, then shared a shrug. They followed Nyrass and Aminza where they walked slowly ahead, the wizard leaning a little on the girl's arm, through a great oaken door and into the castle proper.

In a room high in an east-facing turret, where the sun flooded through great arched windows, they breakfasted on honey and bread washed down with scented tea from Kikuran, simple but satisfying fare. As they ate so the adventurers told their tale and Nyrass listened attentively, occasionally nodding his head. He was done with eating before his guests, and after daintily dabbing at his lips he said:

'Well, most of what you've told me is as I divined it. Indeed I followed part of your flight on the life-leaf in my shew-stone. That, however, was quite by accident and I assure you I haven't been spying on you. No, for I have my own problems and little enough time these days for wizardly pursuits.' He chuckled a little, but sadly, they thought.

'Very well,' he continued after a while, 'you've told your tale so now I'll tell mine – and may you find it just as interesting.

'Let me think now . . . Ah, yes! I'd best start back at the very beginning, in an age undreamed of by anyone living or dreaming in Earth's dreamland today. Now then, you've repeated to me what the Keeper of the Keep told you of the tenth First One: how he went mad and fled the keep, taking with him the three Wands of Power. Well, let me start my part of the story at that point in time, when dreams were very young and the dreamlands full of a primal magic!

'So the mad tenth First One, Klarek-Yam by name, stole the wands and made off with them. Now these wands were the tools of the First Ones – keys, you might call them – the keys of those great gates of space and time through which the First Ones came and went at will. And when the keys were stolen . . . then those gates were locked forever.

'And the Cthulhu-maddened Klarek-Yam knew that he could not keep the wands, not all of them, for the other First Ones had instruments by use of which they would quickly discover their whereabouts if all three were kept together. So, as he fled, the mad one hid the first wand away in a deep cave in the mountains, where long ages later Thinistor found it one day; and the second he tossed into that mighty lake behind the Great Bleak Mountains, so that it was finally washed down into Thalarion and eventually came into the hands of the eidolon Lathi; but the third wand, that one he kept for himself.

'Now, of the wands themselves, let me explain something.

'You have told how Thinistor's wand points the way. Aye, and I may tell you that it has the power to do many other things as well; but indeed pointing the way is its primary function. It is the instrument by use of which the First Ones guided their mighty ships amongst the stars and down the timestreams! And Lathi's wand . . . you have seen how it glows with a cold, golden, everlasting light? That is the essence of the Ultimate Power which propels the ships of the First Ones upon their voyagings. And as for the third wand –

'Ah, but that one is the strangest wand of all!

'By use of the third wand the First Ones are able to slip into and out of this plane of existence, or any other such plane, at will – or they were before it was stolen. It cancels space and time utterly, as if they never were, and reconstructs them to suit itself. Or rather, to suit its masters. Now it has only one master, Klarek-Yam himself, and he is locked in a place where even he cannot use the third and last wand.'

Here Nyrass paused and held up a finger to keep the three silent. 'This, too, shall I explain,' he presently told them; and eventually, after a little thought, he continued with his tale.

'In those primal days of dream there dwelt here beside the Tross, in this very castle, my ancestor Soomus the Seventh of the Seventh. Now as his name and title implies he was the seventh son of the seventh son of dreamland's very first wizard, and as such he was mightier in magic than all other men. How easily he could have made the dreamlands in their entirety his own, had he so desired. He was a good man, however, as have been all of his descendants with very few exceptions.'

'One of those exceptions being Thinistor Udd,' Eldin cut in, a trifle sarcastically.

'Er, aye, even so,' Nyrass agreed and quickly went on. 'Now Soomus kept in the castle's apartments some of dreamland's most ancient and esoteric writings, direful tomes whose very titles may not be spoken by sane or human tongues. I myself have inherited certain of those volumes, and I may tell you that even I *dare not* look into all of them! Suffice it to say that upon the least potent pages one may find Koth's Sign explained and His Essence delineated, the runic keys to the Pnakotic Manuscripts, spells for conjuring the Myriad Minions of Maggab, and numerous other terrible thaumaturgies whose purposes I will not even name.

'Well, the crazed First One had heard of Soomus and knew him for a mighty magician. He determined to seek him out and ask his aid in the performance of the blackest rite of all, which, were it performed, would surely doom Earth's dreamland in its entirety – not to mention the rest of space and time!

'In short, he wished to free Cthulhu and the Great Old Ones from their immemorial prisons – not only here but also in the waking world! Need I say more on that subject? Of course not.

'And so he came to Soomus with his wand and his blasphemous proposition. In the wand, you see, he already controlled the power to seek out and find Cthulhu and his ilk, so that all he needed from Soomus was a key to their prisons, with which to undo in a moment all the work of the Great Gods of Eld. Of course, Soomus and Klarek-Yam, they themselves would not be harmed. No, for they would be first-loved amongst all Cthulhu's human priests and acolytes. And immortal, they would walk in wonder and glory forever!' Nyrass uttered a dry chuckle.

'But who, I ask you, would willingly become an immortal madman? Certainly not my ancestor Soomus the Seventh of the Seventh, you may be sure!

'And so he asked for time to consider the mad one's madder proposal, and instead prepared a potent spell and a trap fit for one so wily as that lunatic First One; and indeed the poor mad creature fell into Soomus's trap, for which we can all be thankful. And Soomus shrank him down, him and his wand and all, and prisoned him in a glass sphere no bigger than a shew-stone. And there he remains to this day – but for how much longer, no man can say . . .'

'To this day?' repeated Hero. 'Alive?'

'Aye, for my ancestor had not the heart to take the First One's life. They are long-lived, the First Ones, as you know, and this coupled with Soomus' spell made Klarek-Yam near-immortal.'

'And the third wand is locked in the shew-stone with him?' questioned Eldin.

'Indeed it is, and many books of magic also, for they were in the rooms which Soomus shrank. He shrank

214

entire rooms, as many as a great house, the better to ease the mad First One's bitter imprisonment.'

The three looked at each other and back at Nyrass. 'It's a strange story for sure,' grunted Eldin, 'and we certainly don't wish to seem ungrateful for your hospitality, but –'

'But you don't believe me anyway, is that it?' the wizard smiled his sad smile. 'Very well, you shall see for yourselves.'

He stood up and beckoned them to follow, leading the way down spiral steps from the turret and out across the courtyard to an iron-bound door of age-blackened oak. There they paused while he took out a great key from his wizard's robe, turning it in the lock of the massive door.

'You seem to take good care of this shew-stone, Nyrass,' said Hero as they descended dank steps into deep bowels of earth. 'Is that where we're going – to see the shew-stone?'

'Yes to both questions,' answered Nyrass. 'I do take good care of it, and you are going to see it. Of course I take good care of it, for if ever Klarek-Yam should escape –' and he shrugged. 'That would be the end of it.'

Now Aminza spoke up, asking: 'And is he likely to escape?'

'I fear so,' Nyrass nodded.

'But if your ancestor Soomus locked him up all those centuries ago,' she pressed, 'why shouldn't you do the same?'

'Soomus took him by surprise, child. And after all these – not centuries, my dear, but eons – d'you really think he'd allow himself to be taken so easily again?' Aminza had no answer, and in another moment the way had grown so dark that she held up Lathi's wand to light the way.

The steps wound interminably down and the air quickly grew colder. Nitrous patches gave the walls a leprous appearance, and the footsteps of the party echoed loudly. Now Eldin thought to inquire: 'You said the mad First One is likely to escape, but you didn't say how he'd go about it. Is someone trying to free him?'

'He is trying to free himself, as he has tried ever since Soomus locked him away,' Nyrass answered.

'That's what puzzles me about your story,' Eldin returned in his rumbling growl. 'If this crazy Klarek-Yam has the third wand with him in his fish-bowl world, how come he's still *in* there at all? I thought the thing was a key to alien dimensions, times and places?'

'So it is,' said Nyrass, nodding his white head and calling a halt as they reached the foot of the stone staircase. 'Indeed it is – but its powers were reduced along with its size!'

'What?' cried Eldin. 'Are we fools that we should believe all this?'

Nyrass paused before a door which was strong as the one at the top of the steps. He turned to Eldin and frowned. 'Dreamer,' he said, 'you persist in doubting my word! Fortunately for you I love my fellow men, even unlovely ones . . . What would you do if I struck you?'

'Eh?' said Eldin, surprised. 'Why, with my temper, I'd probably strike you back!'

'And if you were only one inch tall?'

'An inch?' Again Eldin was taken aback. 'Why, I'd – I'd –'

'And if you were less than a grain of sand?' Nyrass pressed. 'Don't you see? Just as the mad First One was made tiny, so was his power. And so was the power of his wand.'

Hero was frowning heavily and that was a sign that

something bothered him mightily. 'Nyrass,' he said, 'you may well find that Klarek-Yam has an ally in a certain Ossaran, one Ebraim Borak. You'll remember we told you it was Borak sent us into the mountains in the first place to bring back Thinistor's wand. Could it be that Borak plots to release the First One?'

'Ah, no!' replied Nyrass, 'though I can see why you might think so. But no, I myself enlisted Borak's aid in attempting to recover the first wand. I thought the wand might help me to prevent the inevitable escape of the mad First One, do you see? But as an agent the Ossaran was not a good choice. He was too devious, untrustworthy. I later discovered – even as you discovered – that he was in league with Thinistor Udd himself!'

'Aye,' Eldin grunted, 'and we've still a score to settle with Borak.'

'No longer,' Nyrass smiled his wan smile. 'All such scores were settled when Borak ran a-foul of the law in Theelys. He came to me for help, and when I would have hidden him away he attempted to murder me. He had determined, you see, to make himself the next Great Wizard of Theelys. With all of my books, charms, spells and other devices, he just might have succeeded.'

'You killed him?' Eldin seemed disappointed.

'No, for that is not my way.'

'Well, it may not be your way, Nyrass,' Hero cut in, impatient now, 'but we don't have your benevolent nature. Where's Borak now?'

'Come,' answered the ancient magician. 'The answer – all answers – lie within the rooms beyond this door. If you see for yourself, then you will know and understand. Then, too, you'll fear the madness of the tenth First One as much as I do!'

III
THE TENTH FIRST ONE

From the cold, nitrous foot of the stone steps, Nyrass led the questers into brightly lighted, sumptuous subterranean apartments which would rival in their opulence any of the wizard's own rooms in the castle far above. They would never have suspected that such a place could exist down here, and by the neatness of the rooms it was obvious that they were occupied. But by whom? Hero asked this of Nyrass as he led them through one well-kept room after another.

'Why, by my good and faithful servant Ebraim Borak, of course! For this is where I keep my most precious books, my instruments – all of the many appurtenances of wizardry – and I'm too old to keep the place neat and tidy for myself. Ebraim does it for me, and his payment is that I keep him here, safely hidden away from the forces of law and order.'

'Wizard,' Eldin rumbled, 'you've made a big mistake bringing me here, for when I meet up with Borak, I'll –'

'You'll do nothing, my large friend,' said Nyrass, unperturbed. 'Now save your breath and don't argue, for you'll see soon enough that this Ebraim Borak is not the same man who sent you on your fool's quest.'

Eldin might have argued for all the wizard's words, but at that moment a door opened and a green-clad man bustled in, smiling broadly as he saw the four and bowing to them. Then, without a word being spoken, he set about to fill the wells of the room's many lamps where they stood in niches in the walls. All the while he hummed to himself and smiled, exuding an air of pleased satisfaction which was very nearly tangible.

For a long moment the questers stared at the man where he busied himself, then Eldin stepped forward and spun him about. 'Borak!' The scarfaced dreamer's face was a mask of anger as he spat out the other's name. 'Ebraim Borak!'

The smile never left the Ossaran's face for a moment. As Eldin scowled, so Borak smiled, and gradually it dawned on the brawny adventurer that indeed this was not the man he had met in Hymat Zorathin's tavern on the Street of Rats so many nights ago. The same body and face, certainly, but not the same mind. Not *any* mind to speak of!

For Borak's smile was blank as his eyes, and no slightest sign of recognition showed upon his face. Eldin might be the man in the moon for all the Ossaran knew or cared.

Slowly the burly dreamer released Borak, who immediately returned to his task of filling the lamps. Aghast, Eldin turned his suddenly pale face to Nyrass; and the wizard smiled his sad, wan smile and said, 'And are you satisfied now, Eldin the Wanderer? Or would your punishment have been greater than mine?'

No answer came, neither from Eldin nor from the others, and so Nyrass nodded and said: 'Very well . . . Now then, if you will please follow me into the final chamber? And here at last you shall see the shewstone prison of the mad First One.'

The final room had nothing of the opulence of the others. It was the wizard's workshop and made no pretence to be anything else. Benches littered with complicated apparatus were set against two of the cold stone walls; the flags of the floor were of unadorned stone; the ceiling had been blackened in places by strange fires and several supporting columns were stained with oddly-coloured marks and splashes. One wall was covered with scrawled signs and symbols, while another was hung with a great mirror whose bronze frame was of rearing Krakens. But in the very centre of the room – upon a stone table whose base was bolted to the floor – there stood the shew-stone of which Nyrass had spoken, and without preamble he led his guests to it.

The glass globe was smoky-blue, big as a large skull, perfectly round – and completely opaque!

'What?' grunted Eldin, peering into the veiled heart of the globe and seeing nothing. 'What? And is this the supposed home of the tenth First One?'

Letting Eldin peer, Nyrass turned to Hero and Aminza. 'Your friend is a hard man to convince,' he wryly commented, 'but I can understand his disappointment. It must be very hard to have come so far, only to be thwarted at the last.' He turned back to Eldin. 'Would you truly spy upon Klarek-Yam in his globe?' he asked.

'That I would,' replied Eldin, 'if only to be sure he's in there!'

'Very well, it shall be done. I long ago devised a means by use of which I might know what Klarek-Yam was about. Lately I have not used it; frankly, I've feared to learn what fresh marvels he has discovered toward making his escape! But now, since your curiosity demands it –'

He went to a bench and took up a slender, rune-carved rod of wood more nearly the shape and size that the adventurers would expect of a true wand, and with this in hand turned to the great mirror where it hung on its wall. 'The mirror is my window on the tiny world of the mad First One,' he explained, 'and my wand is the cord with which I draw the curtains!' And he tapped gently upon the kraken-adorned glass with the wand's tip.

A thin beam of light so intense as to seem almost a solid shaft of silver leapt the distance from the shew-stone to the mirror, which in the same instant was no longer a mirror but a picture of such marvelous clarity that it seemed the glass itself had become a doorway through which Nyrass and his guests might step into the scene beyond.

The scene itself – when the adventurers had recovered their senses sufficiently to look – was of a room much like the very room in which they stood, with benches and books, chemical and alchemical apparatus, and walls literally covered with scrawled glyphs and symbols of every esoteric connection. And yet no one was present in that room and nothing stirred.

'Oh?' said Eldin after a while, his voice less blustery than normal. 'And where's Klarek-Yam?'

'You see those arched doorways?' answered Nyrass. 'Klarek-Yam is in one of the many rooms beyond. Try not to be impatient, for he rarely absents himself from his experiments for very long. He has only one ambition – to be out of the shew-stone and about his insane task – which means that he must constantly try and try again to find a means by which to free himself. You see all of those great books there? That was Soomus' one oversight: that those tomes of magic were locked in the sphere with Klarek-Yam.'

As Nyrass finished speaking something moved in the shadow of a doorway to the right of the scene, at which the adventurers crowded closer. A figure, manlike in outline, or so it seemed, clad in a hooded robe like the cowled cassock of some monkish order, entered the picture and turned toward a bench whereon a massive, black-bound book lay open at a page of glowing symbols.

Eldin, moving still closer to the mirror, accidentally disturbed a small glass flask where it stood upon a bench. The flask fell to the floor and shattered loudly. Nyrass' guests froze on the instant, but the wizard seemed not at all perturbed.

'He can't hear you,' he told them, 'though certainly he'll see us if he turns this way. He, too, has a mirror, you see, so that this room of mine is transparent to him as his is to me.'

'He looks much like a man, this Klarek-Yam,' said Hero, his voice a whisper despite Nyrass' assurance that the First One could not hear him. 'I did not picture the First Ones as being so . . . manlike?'

'They are not!' said Nyrass with a shudder. 'Be thankful he wears his robe, for beneath it is a monster – at least in our eyes. Be thankful, too, that with this sole exception the First Ones are good as their aspect is evil!'

Even as Nyrass spoke the grey-robed figure in the mirror-room turned and looked directly at the four where they stood. Eldin took a hasty step to the rear as Aminza threw her arms about his burly neck and gave a little shriek. Hero's eyes went wide and the flesh began to crawl on his arms and back. Only Nyrass remained unmoved, and he nodded an accustomed greeting to the creature who gazed out of the mirror at him. Klarek-Yam nodded back, an almost imperceptible movement of his hooded head, and continued to stare.

They could only see the First One's eyes, but that was quite sufficient. They flared and sputtered like yellow pits of hell, those eyes – like great gaping sockets in a skull – and the intensity of their gaze was such that it gnawed at the very souls of the adventurers where they stared back.

'Well,' said Nyrass after a moment, shattering the silence and causing his guests to start in shock, 'and shall we try a little experiment of our own? For I didn't come all the way down here simply to satisfy your curiosity, my young friends. No, indeed. This may be the end of *your* quest, but it's only the beginning of mine.'

'What do you mean, Nyrass?' asked Hero, his voice a little croaky from the sudden clamminess of his mouth.

'Why simply that you've brought me the wands I need to strengthen Soomus' barrier about Klarek-Yam, of course. At least, that is how I plan to use them in the very near future – with your permission?'

Hero and Aminza at once reached inside their shirts and produced their wands, and so swift was their reaction to Nyrass' request that he was given no chance to check them. In any case, his interest still centred upon the figure of Klarek-Yam where the First One stood in his mirror-room, and so he only became aware of their deadly blunder through the immediate change in the visage of the monster beyond the mirror.

'*Not just now!*' cried Nyrass, staggering back away from the kraken-glass, his mouth falling open in horror as he saw the wands in Hero's and Aminza's hands. But already he was far too late.

For as each new descendant of Soomus had become Klarek-Yam's keeper down the eons, so had the mad First One sworn vengeance on the whole human race – in the dreamlands and in the waking world alike. And in all those countless years he had dreamed of this moment many thousands of times; when at last he would be able to use his eon-won dark knowledge to the full through the medium of the Wands of Power!

Thus, in that instant before Nyrass cried out, Klarek-Yam had ripped from his robe the third wand – had produced it and held it up to the mirror in his microscopic apartments in the shew-stone – and at his command there commenced a rapid and irreversible sequence of events.

Beams of silver light flashed from his wand, *through* the mirror, and sped to the wands in the hands of the two adventurers. Hero and Aminza were hurled backward across the room, the wands snatched from them by an irresistible force; and as the silver beams withdrew through the mirror, so the wands went with them. Now Klarek-Yam once more possessed all three wands, and now too he could use them in his eon-plotted fashion.

Lathi's wand would provide the power needed by his own rod to melt the space-time barrier which surrounded him, and Thinistor's wand would guide him through the warp and into the land of Earth's dreams. The crazed First One seemed to swell outward then, filled with a terrible strength. He threw off his robe, held up the wands in triumph, and for one mad moment stood fully revealed – a grey upright slug with corrugated skin and tentacles for arms – before the mirror shivered into a thousand fragments!

As that occurred so Nyrass' shew-stone also disintegrated with a roar that shook the room and tossed wizard and dreamers alike against the walls like so many rag dolls, and when the reverberations of that great blast died away . . . There stood Klarek-Yam, free at last, amidst shattered stone fragments where once the prison crystal had stood upon its table. His tentacles writhed namelessly and his eyes blazed hideously in his slug's head as he peered about the still smoking room; and in a moment his gaze alighted upon the figure of the wizard Nyrass where he struggled to his feet in a littered corner.

'*Nyrass!*' came a great croak like the massed grunting of toads. '*Spawn of Soomus! Now feel the wrath of Klarek-Yam! Now journey where no being or thing ever journeyed before, and never shall again!*'

The alien abomination pointed all three tentacle-wrapped wands at the half-stunned, stumbling wizard – and in that same instant a green-clad figure entered the room, took in the scene at a glance, threw himself headlong between the crazed First One and the helpless form of his master. Unsmiling for once, Ebraim Borak took the full burst of eerie energy which Klarek-Yam now released. For a single instant the Ossaran's outline seemed to pulse and glow – and then his empty green robe crumpled formlessly to the floor!

By now Hero and Eldin were on their feet, swords drawn, their faces fear-drained masks as they staggered toward Klarek-Yam. In their shocked condition they were no threat to the First One and he knew it. He ignored them and re-aligned his wands upon Nyrass. Then –

Klarek-Yam uttered a single, astonished, croaking shriek as the tentacle which held the wands withered, blackened and turned to ashes and smoke in an instant. His other appendages immediately followed suit, and the circular mouth in his rubbery head was all set to frame a second cry when the incredibly swift *corruption* caught up with it also, turning his head to motes of coloured dust. And only a column of writhing, vile-smelling smoke remained where the maniac First One has stood.

The entire – decomposition – of Klarek-Yam's

being had been so rapid that the falling wands had not yet clattered to the floor when the thing was over and done with . . .

'It was Soomus saved us,' Nyrass told them much later, when they had returned to the higher, less claustrophobic regions of the castle. 'And to think I have underrated my ancestor all these many years. I might have known he'd foresee Klarek-Yam's eventual escape and take precautions against it. His method was simple, really. So long as Klarek-Yam remained within his shew-stone prison he was near-immortal, but if ever he left it –'

'All of those unnumbered centuries would catch up with him, eh?' guessed Hero.

'Exactly. And so ancient was the mad First One that he should have been dust a quarter-billion years ago . . .'

'But what of the rest of the First Ones?' queried Aminza. 'The nine who lie sleeping in the great keep high in the mountains? Will they, too, decay and fly into dust when the Keeper rouses them up?'

'No, child, not them,' Nyrass shook his old head. 'The magic which holds them in thrall is the Magic of Science. That of my ancestor Soomus –' he shrugged. 'That was only – magic!'

'Well, well!' said Eldin. 'So Klarek-Yam's bottle-world was nothing really but a miniature Shangri-la, eh?'

'Shangri-la?' frowned Hero, as at hearing the name of some dimly distant, all but forgotten place.

'Er, yes,' said Eldin knowledgeably, but he nevertheless matched Hero's frown. 'It's, er, a valley that lies beyond the Onyx Columns of the South –'

'– You think!' cried Hero and Aminza together, and they all three laughed out loud.

IV
WHEN THE
SLEEPERS WAKE!

They stood atop the castle's tallest turret in the morning sunlight, all three of them clean, bright and rested after four days and nights of leisurely living as Nyrass' guests and at his expense. The wizard would have it no other way, for in his own words the adventurers had given him 'a new lease of life!' Truth to tell, they had given all of Earth's dreamland a new lease of life; or at least extended indefinitely the one it already had. Dreamland – the waking world – the Universe itself owed them a debt, which probably never would be acknowledged and certainly never repaid.

The least Nyrass could do was to offer them his hospitality, which they had gladly accepted for four near-idyllic days. The season of mists was past and the spring sun warm; the castle's gardens were expansive and its grass soft and lush; their apartments had been more than adequately appointed and their food the very best that Nyrass could conjure. Indeed, they believed he *had* conjured it from somewhere, for never before in all the towns and cities of their wanderings had they known the like of such wonderful meats, fruits and wines.

Now, replete and revitalized, packs upon their

backs, they were ready to move on; but the last leg of their journey – their mode of conveyance – was to be the strangest yet. Their nightmare ride on the reed-tree raft, even their flight on the Great Tree's life-leaf would be as nothing by comparison. For this time, with Nyrass' aid, their trip would be sheer magic. Not the magic of wizards and sorcerers, no, but the 'Magic of Science,' the science of the First Ones. Quite simply, they would return to the great keep in the mountains via the three Wands of Power!

As to how this could be achieved: Nyrass gave the adventurers his complete assurance that the trip would be painless, trouble free and instantaneous! One second they would be here atop this high turret, and the next . . . All that was required of Hero and Eldin was that they close their eyes, open their minds and *think* of that secret room deep in the heart of the keep. Nyrass would do his bit, of course (coordinating the effort, so to speak), and the wands – they would do the rest.

Now the three said their farewells to Nyrass (Eldin somewhat edgily, displaying a typically suspicious attitude toward magic, be it scientific or esoteric) and formed a triangle. They linked arms, each holding tight to a wand, and with a final glance at the old magician closed their eyes. The men concentrated on the keep's inner room; Aminza simply centered her mind upon staying with them; and Nyrass unified the forces.

All three adventurers felt a moment's dizziness. They staggered a little, opened their eyes –

– And staggered again, but much more violently this second time!

'*WHO DARES ENTER THE KEEP UNBID-DEN?*' roared the Keeper, the lights of his panel tinged red with anger and moving in jerky agitation.

'OH, NOT YOU AGAIN!' Eldin roared back almost as loudly, though more from shock than bravado.

'For goodness' sake relax, Keeper!' cried Hero, his ears ringing. 'It's only us. Oh, and Aminza, too.'

For a moment there was a sort of stunned silence as the lights on the voice-panel rapidly ran through the entire range of the colour spectrum. Then –

'David Hero and Eldin the Wanderer,' said the Keeper in a kind of half-mechanical astonishment. *'And the girl of whom you spoke, Aminza Anz! You've returned, and not through the door. Which means –'* and the Keeper's voice rose almost to a whine, *'– which means –!'*

Aminza's eyes were wide and worried as she stared all about. 'You'll do yourself an injury!' she was moved to cry. 'Whoever you are . . .'

'An injury!' the Keeper cried in a delirium of colour. *'I'll do myself an injury!'*

'You will!' she asserted, nodding her head.

'That doesn't matter,' answered the Keeper. *'Nothing matters except . . . you have the wands?'*

'We have the wands, yes,' said Hero.

A sudden hiss of compressed air heralded the opening of a small door in the room's central control panel. In the opening thus revealed, electrical fires like miniaturized bolts of forked lightning crackled continuously in a darkness deep as the spaces between the stars. Just inside the door, however, where the metal frame ended and the alien darkness began, three evenly-spaced, empty sockets were visible, holes that merged with the inner nothingness and went . . . nowhere.

'The wands,' urged the Keeper in a blaze of gold and green. *'Place the wands in the sockets, one at a time, starting at the left. First Thinistor's wand –'*

Almost of its own accord, as if the wand moved Hero and not the reverse, Thinistor's wand slotted into its hole and was instantly gripped and held fast. Hero released its knob, jumped back, stood well away from that bottomless pool of darkness and its lightning-flash denizens. And immediately those small lightnings lost something of their aimlessness and crackled more certainly.

'Now the source-wand!' cried the Keeper in a throbbing pulse of purple. *'The wand with the golden glow.'*

Aminza stepped forward, her hand trembling as she placed the naked end of Lathi's wand into its socket – until she too felt the stem gripped as the wand was accepted. Hero caught her as she stepped backward, a little off balance.

'Finally,' the Keeper's voice was now a whisper of dull red and yellow, *'the warp-wand!'*

'No,' answered Eldin, backing away with Klarek-Yam's wand gripped tight in his hand. 'Not yet, Keeper.'

'Do it now – at once!' the Keeper roared in a blaze of white anger.

'And what of your promise?' shouted Eldin in return. 'What of our reward? More to the point, what happens when I place this last wand in its socket?'

'Why, then I wake the sleepers,' said the Keeper. *'As for your rewards – you shall have them, never fear. Now – the wand.'*

Eldin looked at Hero and they both turned to the girl. 'It's what we're here for,' she said.

Again Hero and Eldin exchanged searching looks, but at last the older dreamer stepped forward, approached the open door and held out the third wand. The alien energies were alive now and full of purpose. Crackling in their cave of ultimate darkness, the weird lightnings seemed to guide the stem of Klarek-Yam's wand into its slot, almost snatching it from Eldin's fingers.

The door in the control panel hissed shut with an impossible speed and Eldin, falling back away from it, was grabbed hold of and steadied by his friends. A tremendous rumbling purr now welled up in that room of strange metal, setting the soft-textured floor a-throb beneath their feet. In the wall of the room the great entrance gave a hiss which the dreamers remembered of old, and now the exit gaped open as it had when the Keeper first sent them upon their quest.

'*Go,*' said the Keeper. '*Leave the keep at once.*'

'What?' howled Eldin, outraged almost beyond reason. 'What of your promise?'

'*Ask no questions – simply OBEY!*' ordered the Keeper, his voice full, strong and sure.

'Damn you to hell, Keeper!' cried Hero as he and Aminza dragged Eldin forcibly toward the open portal. 'You lied and cheated and robbed us!'

'*Fools!*' came the Keeper's answer. '*My masters are stirring. Would you wish to be here when they start awake?*'

Now the anger went out of the faces of the dreamers in an instant, was replaced by the pallid mask of fear. To be here when the sleeping First Ones awakened. To see them walk abroad. Benevolent they may well be – but on whose authority? The word of the Keeper? Of an old, friendly wizard in Theelys? And their almost limitless power, their utter alienage . . .

'*GO!*' roared the Keeper again as they crossed the door's threshold and it hissed shut behind them; and in the exterior tunnel the echo of that final command, co-mingled with the steadily increasing hum and throb, came back to them again and again where they trembled in darkness.

'Stand still both of you,' grunted Eldin, recovering from his rage. He slipped out of his pack, found his firestones and quickly fashioned a torch of rags tied to the blade of his straight sword. Then, by the uneven light of Eldin's makeshift brand, the three set about to make their exit from the keep.

Knowing the way – urged on by a rumbling which set the entire keep shaking, and by the thought of the First Ones, probably awake and moving in the keep even now – they made light work of the maze of pit-falls and traps. Suddenly speed was of the essence, and the faster they went the faster they wanted to go. Mercifully the gravity-pit had lost its dreadful pull, so that they were able to cross its bone-strewn, previously muscle-wrenching valley at a run; and Eldin's expertise with a tossed grapple never faltered when they reached the far wall.

Then more of the maze, and the lighting of a second torch; more pitfalls and pivoting slabs and echoing rock-cut tunnels; and the rumbling growing to a roar of barely-constrained power, and pictures in the minds of the three of sentient, corrugated, upright grey shapes with yellow pits for eyes and – what? – for souls. And at last the blessed light, and the vertiginous climb down to the surface of the plateau; and for all their haste never a slip or a foot wrongly placed as they completed the climb and set off at a breathless, stumbling run for the cave under the overhang, where once they had battled Thinistor Udd and the monstrous living idol he worshipped.

And finally, as they ran, so Hero gasped out what all three were thinking. 'We're fools, *fools!* What did we ever really know, eh? The tenth First One, mad: Well, he may have been – but who can say for certain? What *is* madness to a First One anyway?'

'You're right, lad,' Eldin grunted. 'For all we

know, Klarek-Yam might have been the only sane
one!'

'And mad or sane, how do we know how the nine
feel about Klarek-Yam?' gasped Aminza. 'I mean – I
mean –'

'We know what you mean, Aminza,' said Hero.
'We killed him – or at least we had a hand in it.'

Now, where the overhang of the cliffs sheltered
them, they stopped running and turned to look back
at the Keep of the First Ones. Even at that distance the
rumbling could be heard and faint tremors reached
the adventurers through the plateau's rock. Great
boulders were dislodged from the keep's face and
thundered down onto the shuddering plateau's shelf
like so many pebbles. The very air seemed to jounce
and tremble, and dust-devils rose up everywhere in
weirdly-dancing spirals.

'Look!' gasped Aminza a moment later, but her
companions were already looking –

– And the hair on their heads prickled in preter-
natural dread as down from the keep snaked something which they had thought never to see again,
something last seen here in this very spot at the end of
the running battle with Yibb-Tstll. It was a greenly
weaving ribbon of light, a snakelike stream of glowing, phosphorescent particles that moved like a
blindworm over and across the vast rocky shelf. Nodding, the 'head' of the eerie stream came to an abrupt
halt as it crossed the path taken by the adventurers
when they ran from the keep.

Then the throats of the three grew dry, for like
some great hound on the trail of blood the blindly
glowing snake of green light began to follow their
track, moving faster as it sped toward them across the
plateau. In another moment it reared over them,
dipped – enveloped them!

'*You are fearful,*' said a voice from nowhere, a voice sweet and gentle as Klarek-Yam's had been harsh and evil, an ethereal yet vibrant voice which seemed to have its source all about them and inside them at one and the same time. '*We do not wish you to be afraid. The Keeper made certain promises. They shall be kept. Eldin the Wanderer – what do you most desire?*'

'Me?' Eldin licked his lips and nervously thumbed his chest. 'You want to know what I –'

'*Come, come, Eldin! Name your reward,*' commanded the voice.

Slowly the older dreamer's eyes widened and a grin spread over his face. 'I want –' he began.

'*Riches?*' prompted the voice.

'No,' he slowly shook his head. 'I've no real use for riches. I want . . . a city at my feet! Where the people will love me, the lords greet me as an equal, and the younger men –' (and he glanced at Hero), 'envy me!'

'*Is that all? Then you shall have it – soon. And you, Aminza Anz? What is your wish?*'

'Only to go back where I belong,' she answered immediately and in a small voice.

'*Where you belong?*'

'Home,' she nodded.

'*You too shall have your wish – soon. And you, David Hero? How may we reward you? – but be quick, for we may not linger here now.*'

'I want . . . a dream-name!' said Hero.

'*Nothing more?*'

'Nothing,' he shook his head. 'I'm sick of being just . . . just any old dreamer! I feel I'm a part of Earth's dreamland now, and so want to belong . . .'

For a moment there was only the weaving of the green glow all around, and then that all-enveloping voice said: '*You are three rare people, and through*

*your actions all of your dreamland is safe once more.
You are adventurers, but more than that you are
heroes. Real heroes . . . You desire a dream-name,
David? Very well, you shall have one . . .'* The voice
paused for a moment and Hero waited expectantly.

*'Occasionally, rarely, a man from the waking
world is allowed to keep his waking name for proper
use in Earth's dreamland. So be it. Henceforth you
shall be David Hero – Hero of Dreams!'*

The green light disappeared, blinked out in a
moment and left the three stumbling on a plateau
which trembled and shook as if in the grip of an earthquake. They hung onto each other, gazed at the keep,
saw the gigantic crack that widened all along the sides
of its base. More boulders tumbled loose and fell
thunderously from keep to rock-strewn shelf. And the
keep – that entire titanic cube of rock – lifted slowly
into the air in a massive shimmering of energy. One
moment it was there, clear of the ground by at least a
quarter of its own height and still rising, and the
next –

Gone!

'Gone!' Hero gasped. 'Back through the gates.'

'They used the wands,' growled Eldin, 'the keys we
brought them.'

'Gone,' whispered Aminza. 'But gone where?'

Although they stood for a long while and stared
across the flat and empty plateau, Aminza's question
remained unanswered.

EPILOGUE

Hero rode from Ilek-Vad along the shore of the Twilight Sea. He rode alone and sadly. Sad for all that his yak was a fine, strong beast and its saddle of tooled leather with silver trappings; and despite the fact that his robe was new and rich, his saddle bags fully provisioned and his purse crammed with gold. He was a man alone, whose only desire had been to belong.

He cast back in his thoughts, remembering the journey which had brought him and his friends through the spring and into the summer, and all across dreamland to Ilek-Vad. There Aminza's foster family had greeted their long-lost child deliriously, Eldin with open arms, and Hero with the greatest kindness and hospitality. Then Eldin had received his reward, with all Ilek-Vad at his feet and his name on the lips of the city's thousands. Eldin the Wanderer, who had brought back Aminza Anz, one of Ilek-Vad's rarest flowers, long-stolen by a night-gaunt.

And Aminza: she had received her reward, too, hadn't she? She was home now, back where she belonged . . .

Hero had not stayed for the wedding, he found reasons enough to refuse the honour of being best man, and no one had seen him slip away. At least he had his dream-name, and a name to be proud of at that. Hero of Dreams . . . Cold comfort.

239

He reined in and stared a while down from silicon cliffs into the deep waters of the Twilight Sea. The bearded and finny Gnorri swam down there, flitting shadows that worked unceasingly on their submarine labyrinths. They were strange and they were silent, but they were not alone.

Hero turned his yak's head back to the trail, and as he did so a distant stirring of dust attracted his eyes. Way back on the track he had taken from the city, heading his way, a rider stood up in the saddle and waved frantically. A fellow traveller, most likely, who sought company along the way. Hero desired no company. Companions were insubstantial things that came and went like moon-shadows on a cloudy night. He looked ahead, not back, and spurred his yak to greater speed. Then a cry reached his ears on the still noonday air and he quickly reined in.

He still didn't look back at the distant speck which grew larger behind him. He didn't look, didn't believe. His ears were playing him false. They must be. And again the cry: a hoarse, distance-thinned shout. Now, recognizing the voice, his heart gave a great leap inside him. He turned at last, screwed up his eyes against the bright summer sun, and –

Yes, he was right. It couldn't be, but it was –

Eldin . . .

Officer Commanding
Traffic Section,
Edinburgh Central.

MAJOR TRAFFIC ACCIDENT
Addendum to Police Report: TA 271/'79

Sir,

The report under cover of the above reference should now be transferred to the 'Fatal Section' and amended as follows:

1. David Hero: injuries, fatal.
2. Prof. Leonard Dingle: injuries, fatal.

Both the above named survived the accident for almost a fortnight but neither regained consciousness.

An interesting fact, however, in respect of Prof. Dingle. On his admittance to intensive care immediately after the accident, it was discovered that he had advanced cancer of the lungs. His post-mortem, just two weeks later, showed his lungs to be completely clear of diseased tissue! The doctors have no explanation.

3. Zaza Inman: no longer on the seriously ill list.

You may remember that Miss Inman (Zaza is believed to be her professional name) was a passer-by, a pedestrian, at the time of the accident. She sustained head injuries when she was struck by a wheel from Prof. Dingle's shattered car. I am pleased to report her partial recovery, in that she regained consciousness yesterday evening. We now think that she was working part-time with a visiting repertory company during the Edinburgh Festival.

Enquiries are now in progress toward tracing a friend of hers, a Mr. Eldin, possibly David Eldin, whose name she frequently repeated while semiconscious. When he is found we shall know more about her. Meanwhile she makes excellent progress.

Sgt D Elliot,
Officer i/c,
Traffic Group 'B'
Edinburgh Central.

THE END

ELF DEFENCE

A magical new fantasy by the
author of
NEW YORK BY KNIGHT

ESTHER M. FRIESNER

WHEN MAGIC MEETS MORTAL

**When Amanda Taylor and her stepson, the elf
prince Cassiodoron, fled Elfhame for the
mortal lands of Earth, Cass's father Kelerison,
Lord King of Elfhame Ultramar, swore he'd hunt
them down and bring them back.**

**Now he's found them . . . and their haven in
the peaceful town of Godwin's Corners faces
invasion by the not-so-peaceable Fair Folk.
But all is not well in Elfhame — and soon
Amanda, Cass and their unlikely allies find
themselves caught up in a struggle for the elfin
throne itself . . .**

ELF DEFENCE

**When magic meets reality anything can
happen.**

FICTION/FANTASY   0 7472 3243 1   £2.99

PAT MURPHY

THE FALLING WOMAN

"A wonderful and literate
exploration of the dark moment
when myth and science meet."
Samuel R Delany

"I dreamed that night, strange, vivid
feverish dreams. I remember dancing in the
rain, holding an obsidian blade. The moon
shone down, almost full, and I was young
again. My robes swirled around me.
A feeling of power surged through me,
a great ancient power that stemmed from
the moon".

Elizabeth Butler is an archaeologist with the ability to see
the ghosts of the past, the lingering remains of the people
who once lived in the ruins she excavates. On a dig in the
Yucatan, she encounters Zuhuy-kak, the spirit of a
long-dead priestess, and comes face to face with the proof
of an ancient Mayan magic – and a conflict of souls that
has survived a millennium.

Elizabeth is trapped between the shadows of a present
that disowns her and a lost, blood-stained past that can be
reborn with the power of her faith – and the strength
of her madness.

"Murphy's sharp behavioral observation, her rich Mayan
background and the revolving door of fantasy and reality
honourably recall the novels of Margaret Atwood".
Publishers Weekly

FICTION/FANTASY   0 7472 3076 5   £2.95

Headline books are available at your bookshop or newsagent, or can be ordered from the following address:

Headline Book Publishing PLC
Cash Sales Department
PO Box 11
Falmouth
Cornwall
TR10 9EN
England

UK customers please send cheque or postal order (no currency), allowing 60p for postage and packing for the first book, plus 25p for the second book and 15p for each additional book ordered up to a maximum charge of £1.90 in UK.

BFPO customers please allow 60p for postage and packing for the first book, plus 25p for the second book and 15p per copy for the next seven books, thereafter 9p per book.

Overseas and Eire customers please allow £1.25 for postage and packing for the first book, plus 75p for the second book and 28p for each subsequent book.